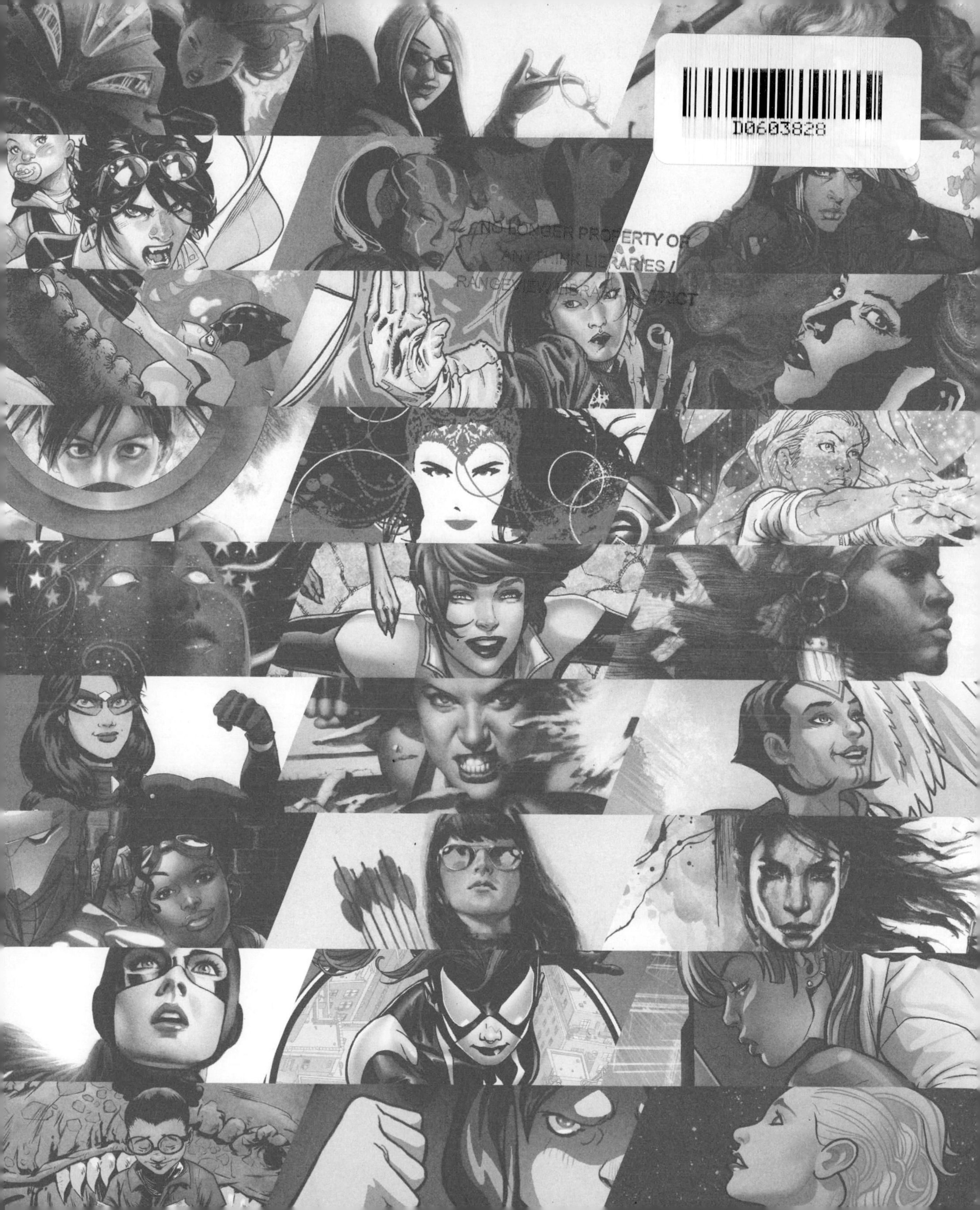

FEARLESS AND FANTASTIC!

Female Super Heroes Save the World

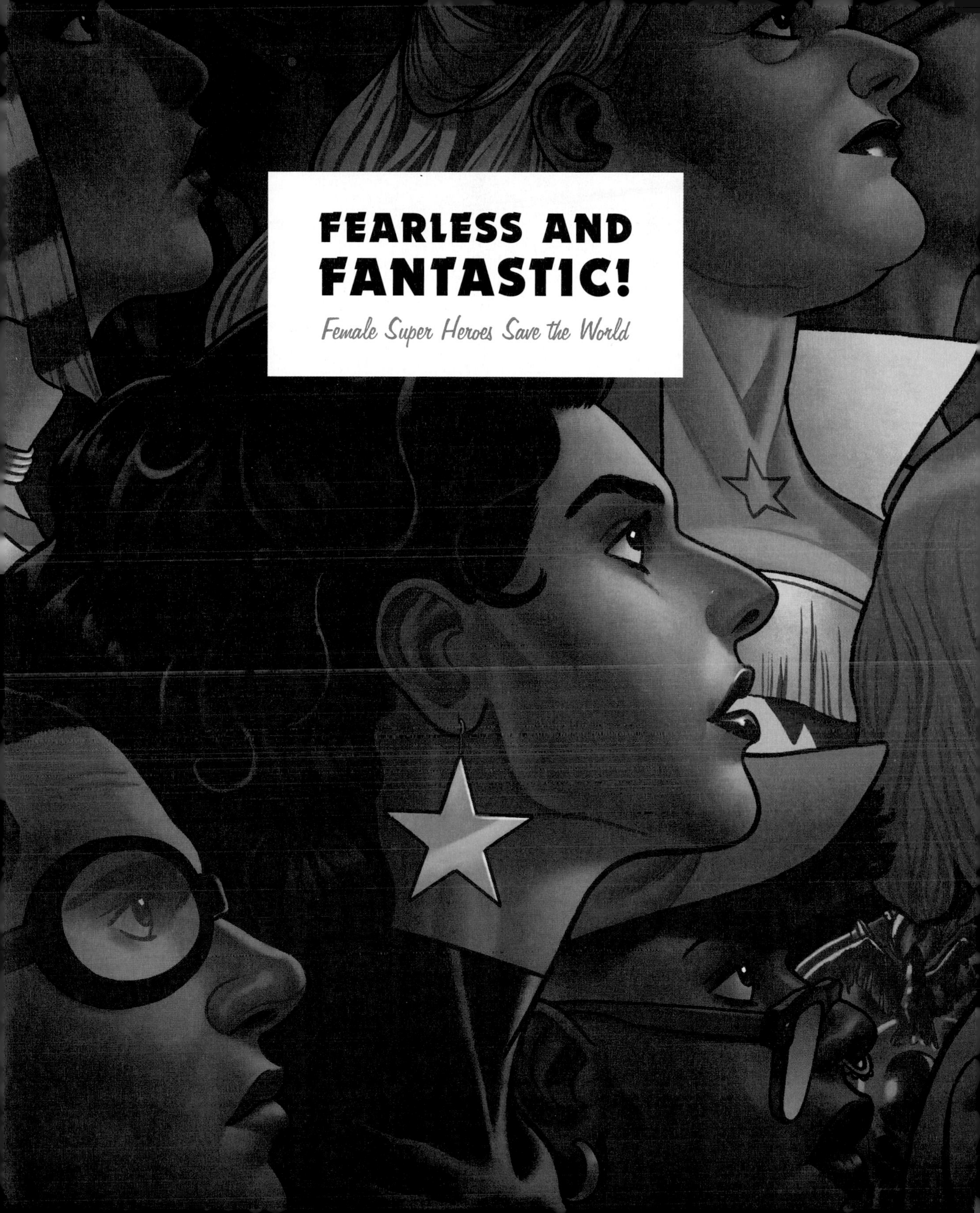

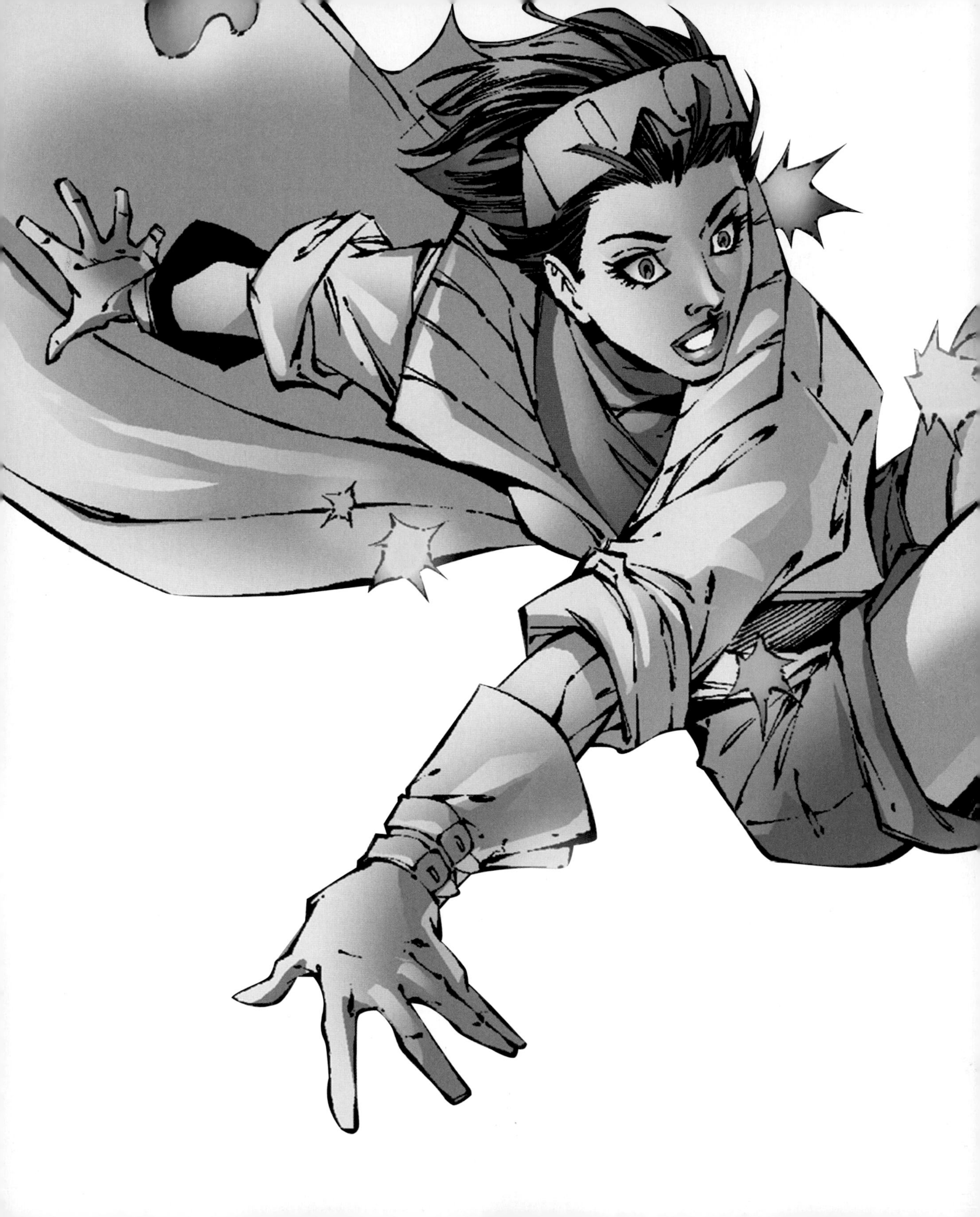

FEARLESS AND FANTASTIC!

Female Super Heroes Save the World

Written by Sam Maggs,
Emma Grange, and Ruth Amos

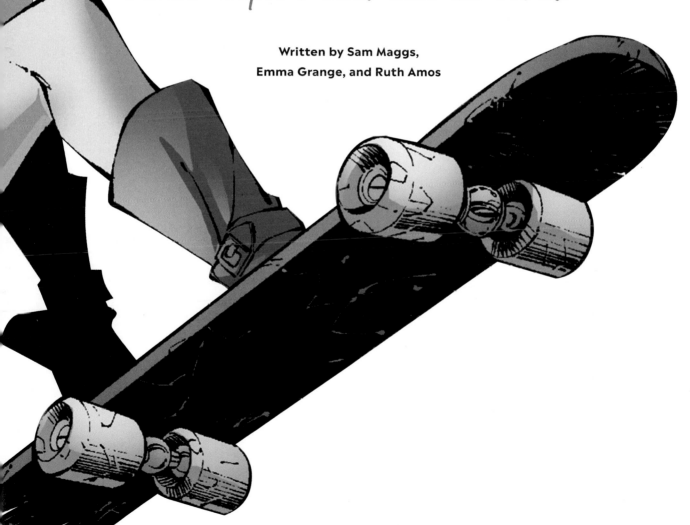

CONTENTS

FOREWORD

My first Super Heroes were powerful women.

As a kid I often felt vulnerable and powerless in the world—the very opposite of what I found in female Super Heroes. Instead their stories were epic and empowering, dangerous and daring—and ultimately—their stories changed my life.

While I knew from a young age that I wanted to be a writer, it was only when I discovered female Super Heroes in the pages of comic books that I was able to imagine what my future as a writer of powerful characters might look like, and what that could mean, not just for me, but to others coming up behind me.

Eventually my stories were filled with the same complex and fascinating women that had originally inspired me as a reader. I've had the chance to write so many of the fearless and fantastic women that grace these gorgeous pages—the iconic all-female Avengers team of A-Force; the sassy private eye sharpshooter Hawkeye; the tenderhearted powerhouse Rogue; and even the hard-boiled detective Jessica Jones. And of course, let us never forget Captain Marvel, the first character I ever got to write for Marvel, and the character whose own squad of pilots, the "Carol Corps," were actually inspired by her devoted real-world fans of the same name.

My journey writing these fictional women also brought me something I never expected—relationships with the incredible *real-life* women of Marvel—the women behind the scenes that make those characters possible. One of those women is Sana Amanat, editor, and now Vice President of Content and Character Development. Her job is to literally shape the future of Marvel Comics, and more to the point, the future of the fearless and fantastic heroes that thrive there.

Thanks to women like Amanat, my first Super Heroes were powerful women, and I'm confident my last Super Heroes will be, too.

Kelly Thompson, writer of heroes

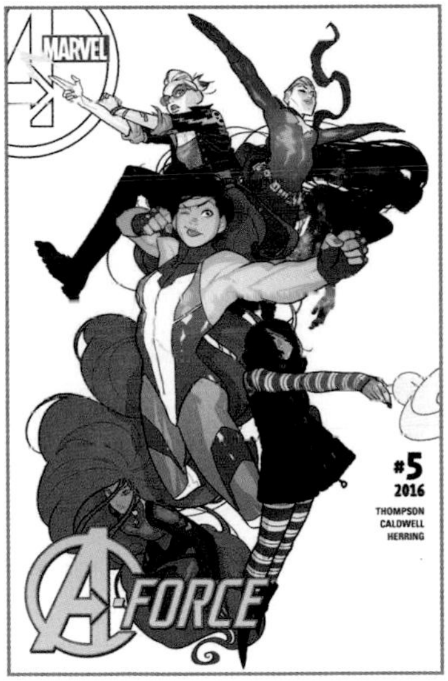
MARVEL
#5
2016
THOMPSON
CALDWELL
HERRING
A-FORCE

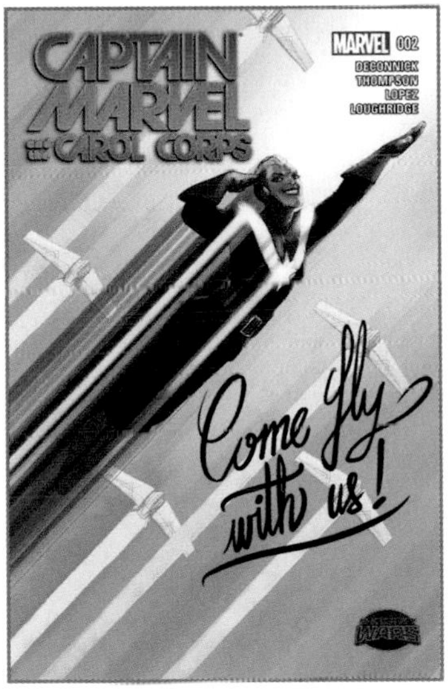
CAPTAIN MARVEL
AND THE CAROL CORPS
MARVEL 002
DECONNICK
THOMPSON
LOPEZ
LOUGHRIDGE
Come fly with us!

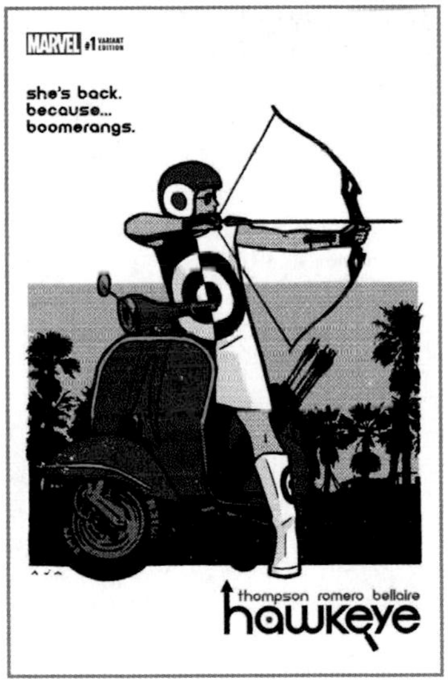
MARVEL #1
she's back.
because...
boomerangs.
thompson romero bellaire
hawkeye

Comic books written and co-written by Kelly

You can find Kelly's fearless, fantastic favorites on these pages:
Captain Marvel (p12), **Nico Minoru** (p30), **Jessica Jones** (p34), **America Chavez** (p56), **Hawkeye** (p58), **Rogue** (p78), **Medusa** (p92), **Singularity** (p94), **She-Hulk** (p106)

INTRODUCTION

Students, warriors, secret agents, inventors, crime fighters, journalists ... the inspiring female Super Heroes of Marvel Comics make their marks in many different ways. Some girls and women are born with super-powers; some gain them by accident or experiment; others have none, and use education, training, or sheer willpower to forge their own paths. But all of these heroes can save the world.

To help readers navigate this book, the characters are arranged into four chapters relating to personal qualities: determination, daring, compassion, and curiosity. Each character may possess a combination, or all, of these qualities; the chapter they appear in indicates that they are a particularly good example of that strength.

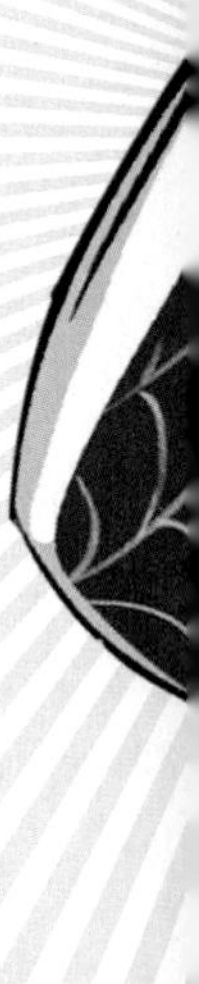

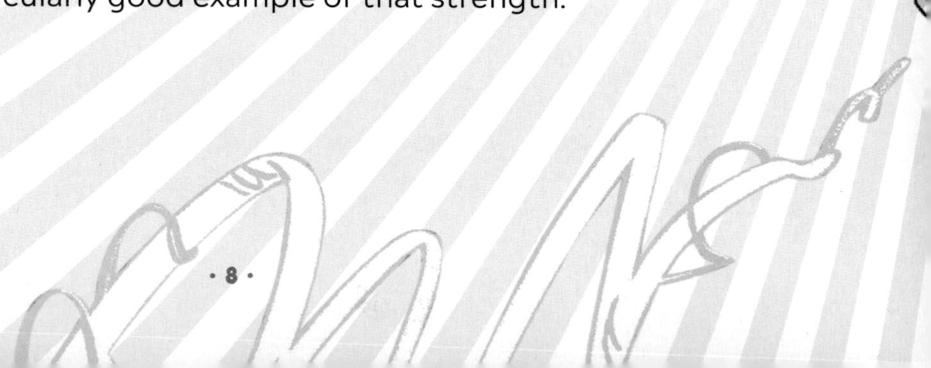

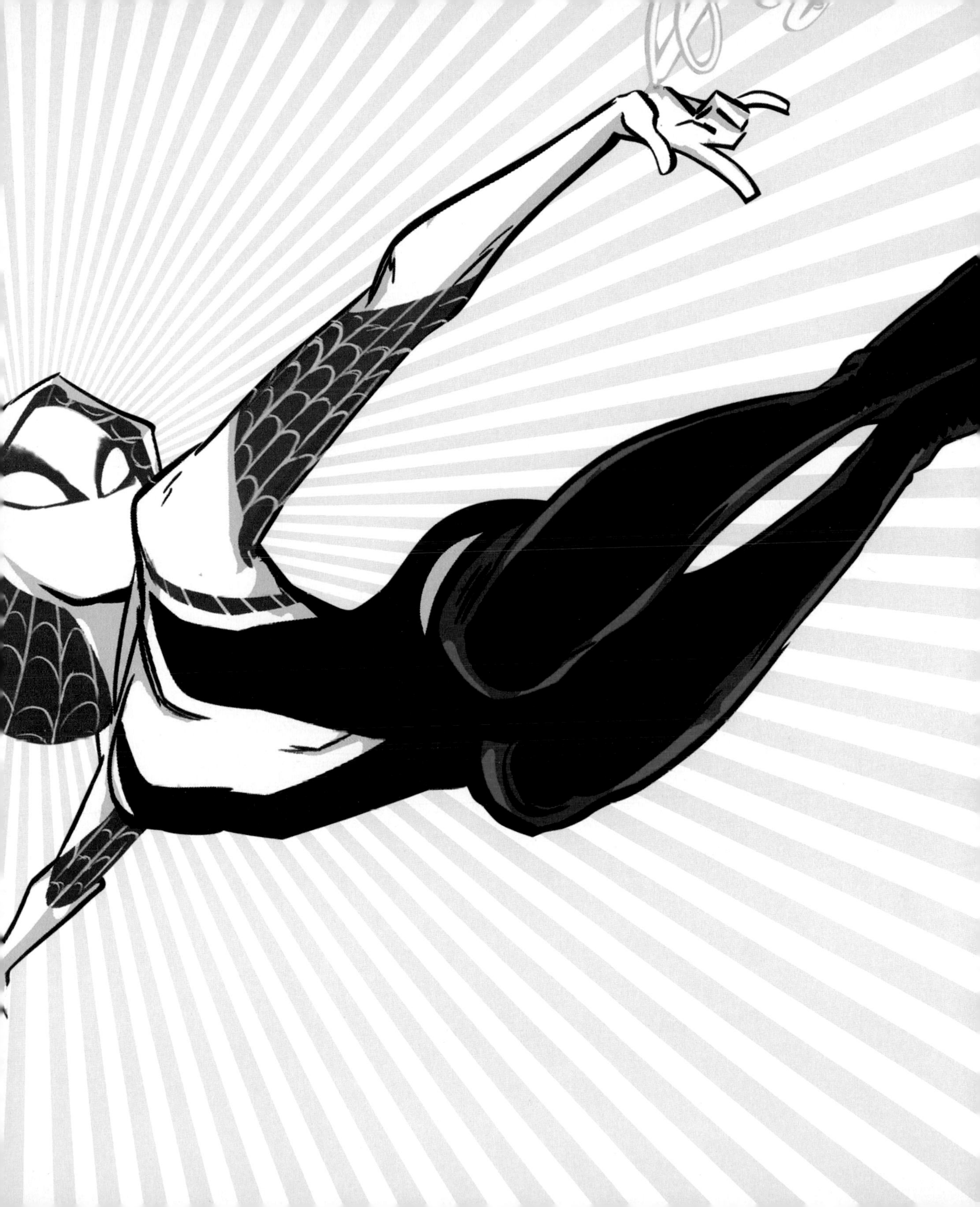

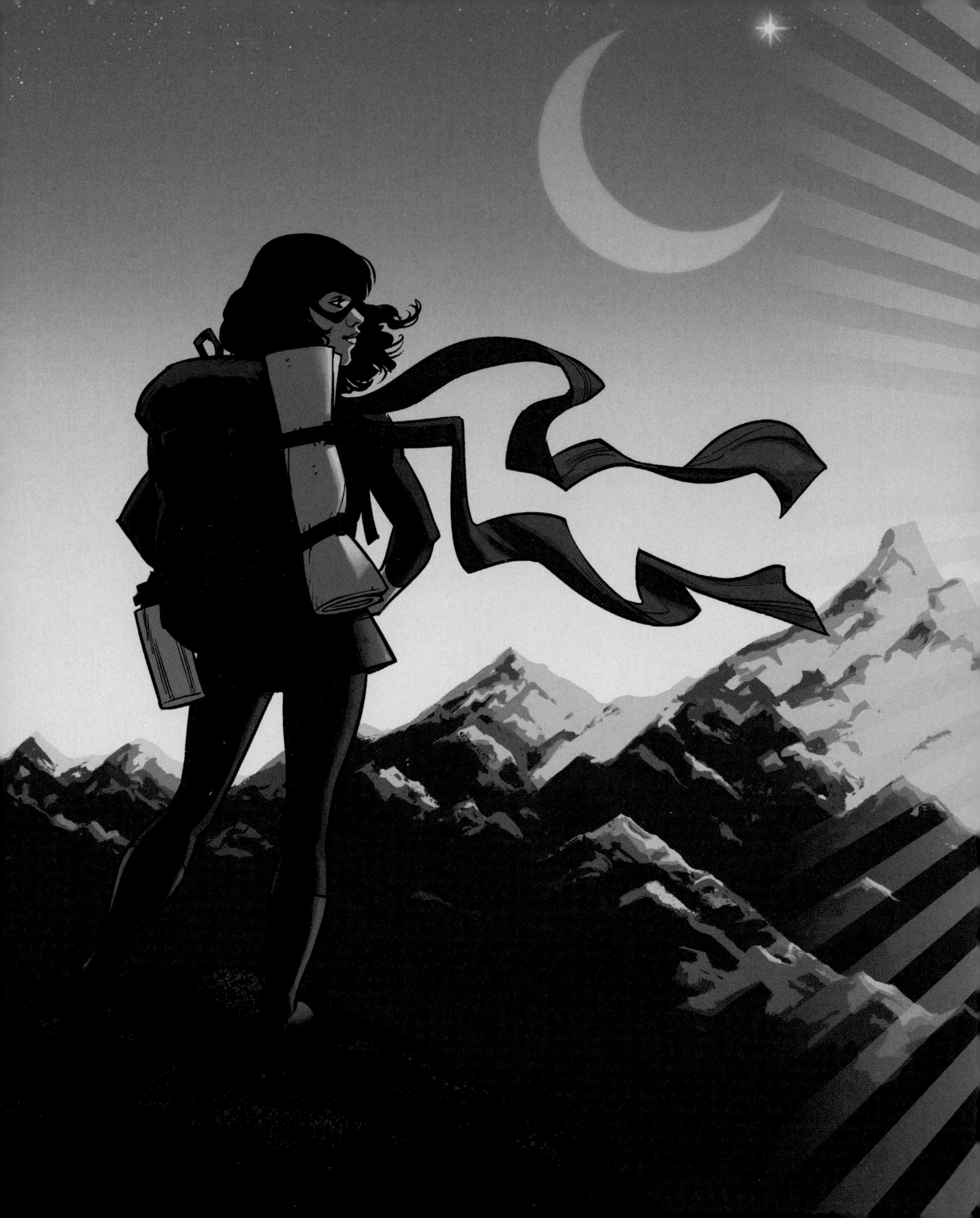

DETERMINED

No matter how challenging things may be, or how much they have to sacrifice to do what is right, these girls and women know that hard work and perseverance will always pay off. Captain Marvel, Silk, Valkyrie, Hellcat—all are driven, strong-willed leaders in their own ways, and all are determined never to take "no" for an answer.

◄ Ms. Marvel (p26)

CAPTAIN MARVEL

"This isn't a question of what I'm not. This is a question of who I could be."

United States Air Force Officer Carol Danvers developed superhuman abilities after she was caught in the blast of an exploding alien device, together with a Kree alien named Mar-Vell. The fusion of their DNA turned Carol into a Kree-human hybrid. In addition to her already phenomenal piloting and military skills, Carol gained superhuman strength and stamina, the power of unaided flight, and the ability to fire energy blasts from her hands. Originally taking the Super Hero name Ms. Marvel, Carol was later known as Binary and Warbird, before adopting the name Captain Marvel.

Fiercely determined and sometimes stubborn, Carol has served as a member of the Avengers, as well as exploring space with the Guardians of the Galaxy group. Making use of her alien experience, Captain Marvel has led the space organization Alpha Flight, responsible for protecting Earth from extraterrestrial threats. The self-proclaimed "boss of space," Carol is also a talented journalist and owns an alien cat named Chewie.

Friends, allies, and role models:
Ms. Marvel (p26), **Jessica Jones** (p34), **Spider-Woman—Jessica Drew** (p102)

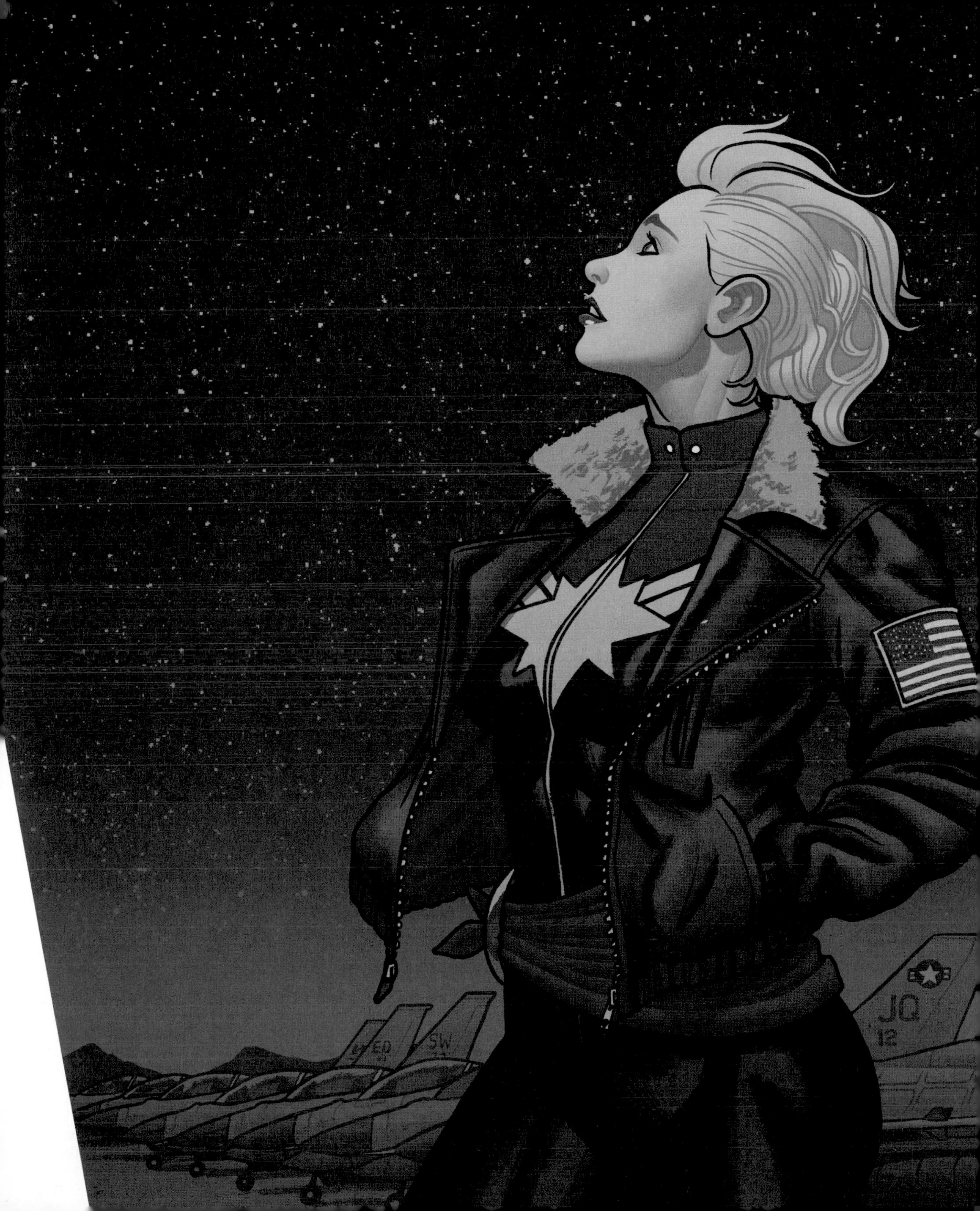
SW
JQ
12

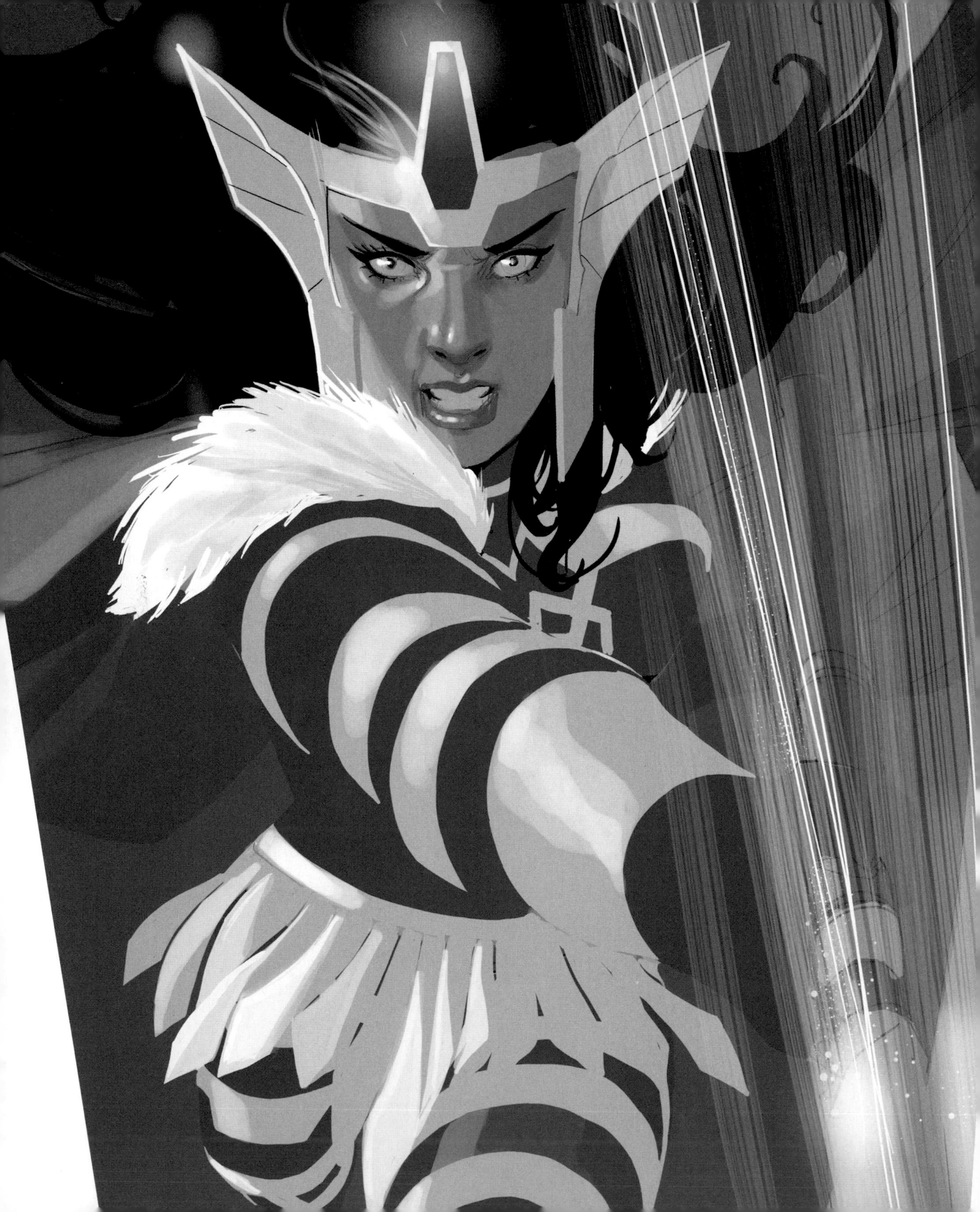

SIF

"Born a **goddess** and forged a **warrior**. I have been **baptized** in the tears of my enemies."

Sif is a fierce Shield Maiden and goddess from the realm of Asgard. She bears an enchanted sword that can slice open passageways between realms. Loki, god of mischief, was jealous of Sif's childhood friendship with his brother, Thor, and cut off Sif's natural golden locks; she has been raven-haired ever since. Sif trained in the ancient Asgardian art of the Berserker, learning special incantations to maximize her devastation on the battlefield. Among Asgardian warriors, only Sif's friend Valkyrie has comparable battlefield skills. With her agility and speed, Sif easily conquers much larger foes.

Although she doesn't fully understand why humans are so important to her fellow Asgardians, Sif has occasionally agreed to assist Earthlings such as medic Jane Foster. She has also been regent of Asgard while King Odin was in his Odinsleep, and is driven by her desire to become a better warrior. Sif never liked that the inscription on Thor's famed hammer, Mjolnir, implied that only men were worthy of lifting it. Notably, the hammer has since modified itself to fix this error.

Friends, allies, and role models:
Valkyrie (p28), **Thor—Jane Foster** (p50), **Peggy Carter** (p54)

STORM

"Queen. Goddess. Cloud-Walker. I think those are too many titles for one who simply wishes to help."

Ororo Munroe is a mutant who can control the elements that create weather, including temperature, water, and electricity. She hails from a long line of priestesses and sorceresses who have white hair, and blue eyes that turn white while using their magical powers. After she manipulated weather on the dry Serengeti Plain to encourage crops to grow, many local tribes came to see Ororo as their goddess of life. It was there that Ororo was recruited into the X-Men team to do good on a worldwide scale. Taking the name "Storm," she bonded especially with Jean Grey and Kitty Pryde as they fought their enemy Magneto and his cunning schemes.

Storm and King T'Challa, aka Black Panther, were once married, and Storm ruled the country of Wakanda alongside him as queen. Storm has also been a longtime leader of the X-Men and the Xavier Institute, and has remained true to her vow to never kill another human. She is one of the most powerful and influential women on Earth.

Friends, allies, and role models:
Misty Knight (p60), **Jean Grey** (p86), **Kitty Pryde** (p116)

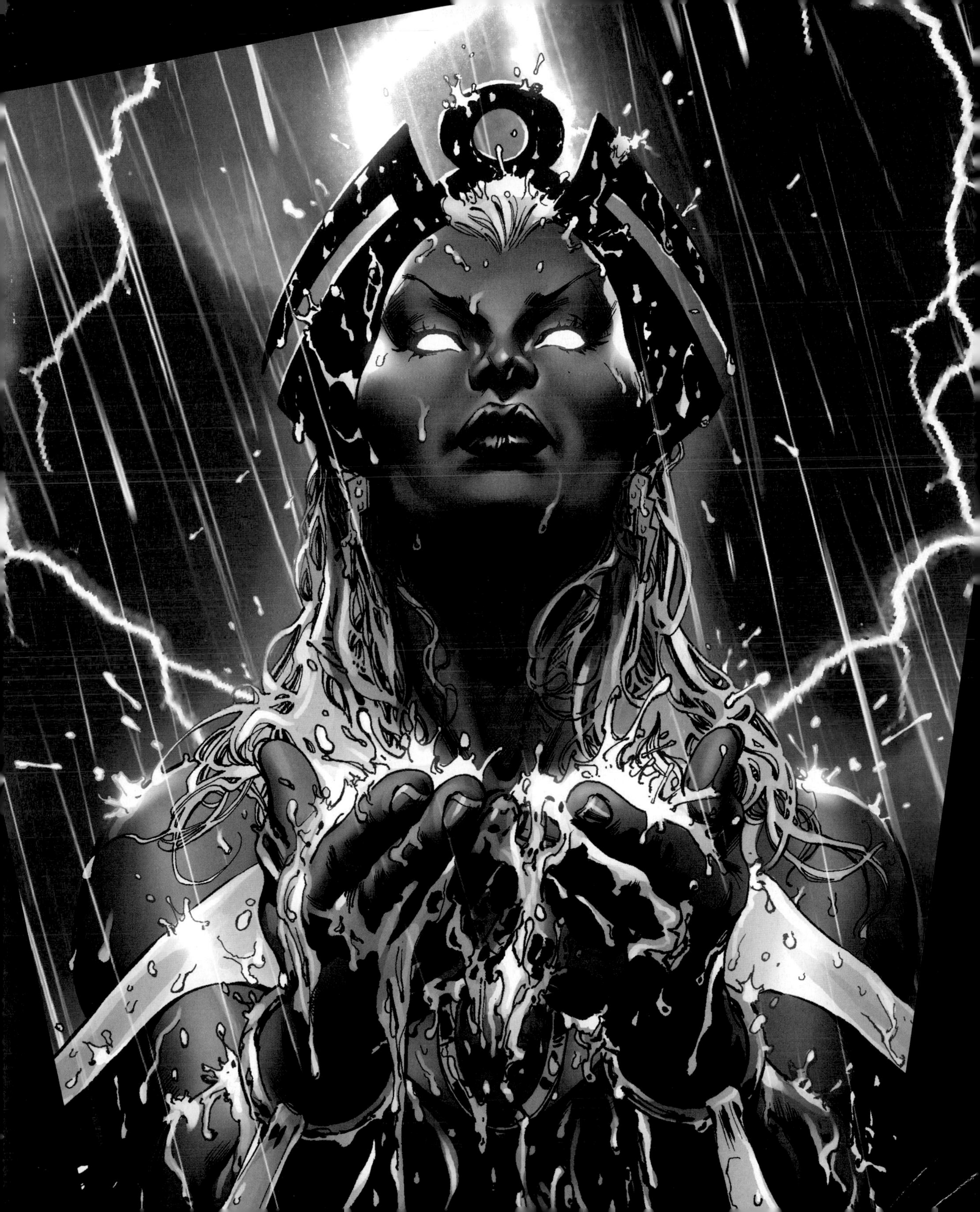

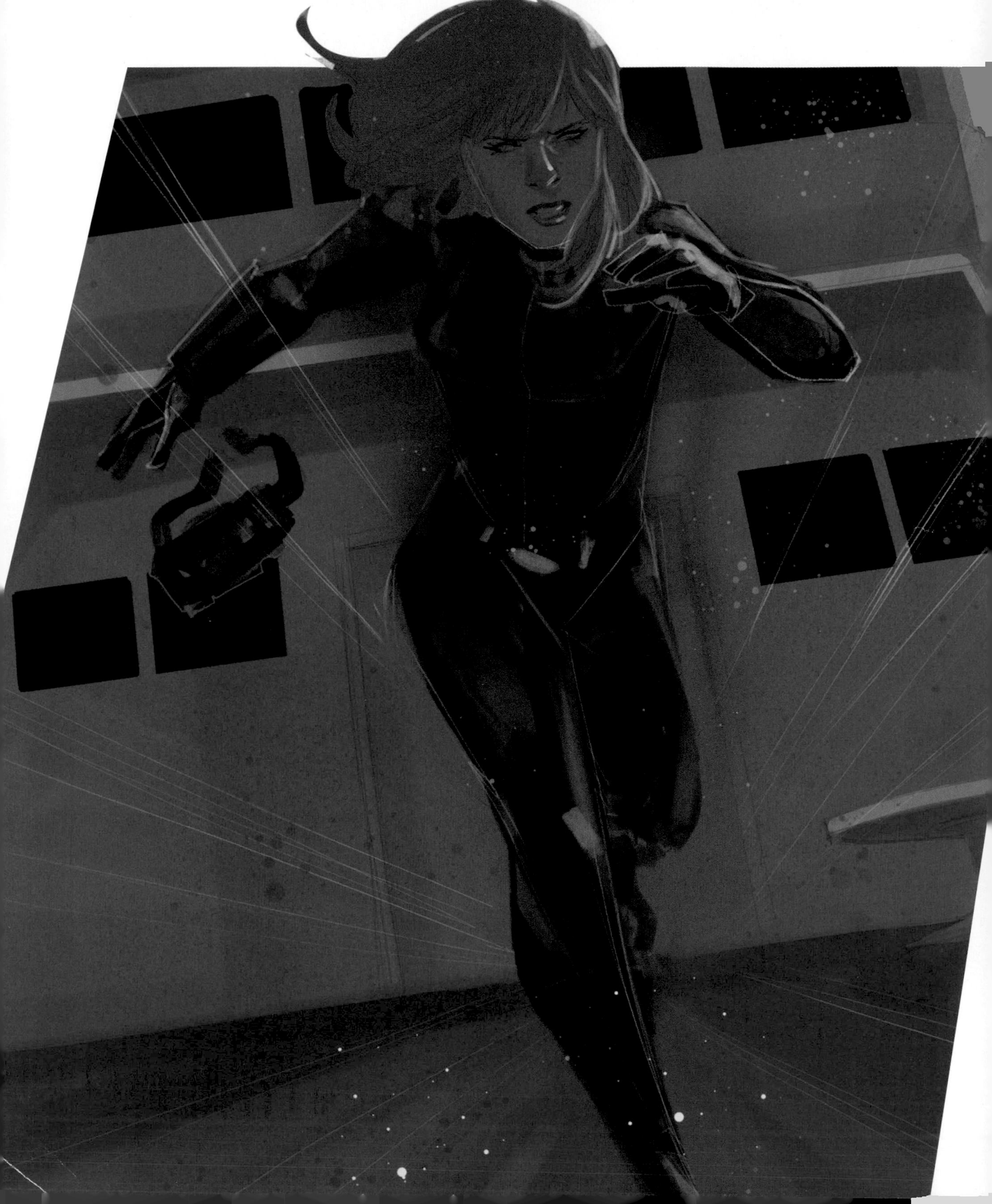

BLACK WIDOW

"This is what I am now. And you'll never know who I was before."

Natasha Romanoff is a Russian former assassin who is now an accomplished member of the Avengers. She was raised in the Red Room, a Soviet Union training facility for girls, where she was trained by agents—including the warrior Winter Soldier—in espionage, combat, and acrobatics. Tricked into believing she had once been a student ballerina, Natasha was recruited as a deadly officer of the KGB, the Soviet Union's security force. She became the Black Widow, fighting against the Super Hero Iron Man until she overcame her brainwashing and fled to the United States.

Black Widow was also biologically enhanced in the Red Room, reaching peak human fitness with heightened strength, speed, and accelerated healing. She wears gauntlets that hold everything from grappling hooks to tranquilizer darts. Natasha's spy skills are unmatched, including mastery of linguistics, infiltration, and hacking. She has worked as an agent of the intelligence group S.H.I.E.L.D. Despite her dislike of making friends, Natasha does keep a cat named Liho, whom she adopted after it refused to leave her apartment.

Friends, allies, and role models:
Valkyrie (p28), **Sharon Carter** (p42), **Quake** (p64), **Pepper Potts** (p90)

HELLCAT

"I think I get it. I'm done running. I'm ready to be a hero again."

Patricia (Patsy) Walker was a model who got caught up in one of the Avengers' missions. The Avengers' training transformed her into a skilled martial artist and hero named Hellcat. She later gained powers that allow her to sense mystical energy, form a personal force field, and summon her costume (complete with retractable claws) at will. But after belonging to both the Avengers and Defenders, Patsy decided on a career change. After working as an investigator at She-Hulk's private law firm, she formed her own business, the Patsy Walker Temp Agency. Not every person with powers wants to be a Super Hero, and so Patsy finds careers and temporary work outside of crime fighting for those people.

Patsy is also a comic book character! Her mother Dorothy, a writer, created a series of romance comics starring teenaged versions of Patsy and her sometimes best friend, sometimes enemy, Hedy Wolfe. The series was incredibly popular for more than a decade. Although Patsy has always felt a little strange about being a fictional character, she still has a love for comic books and the Super Heroes who star in them.

Friends, allies, and role models:
Jubilee (p40), **Spectrum** (p52), **Firebird** (p88), **She-Hulk** (p106)

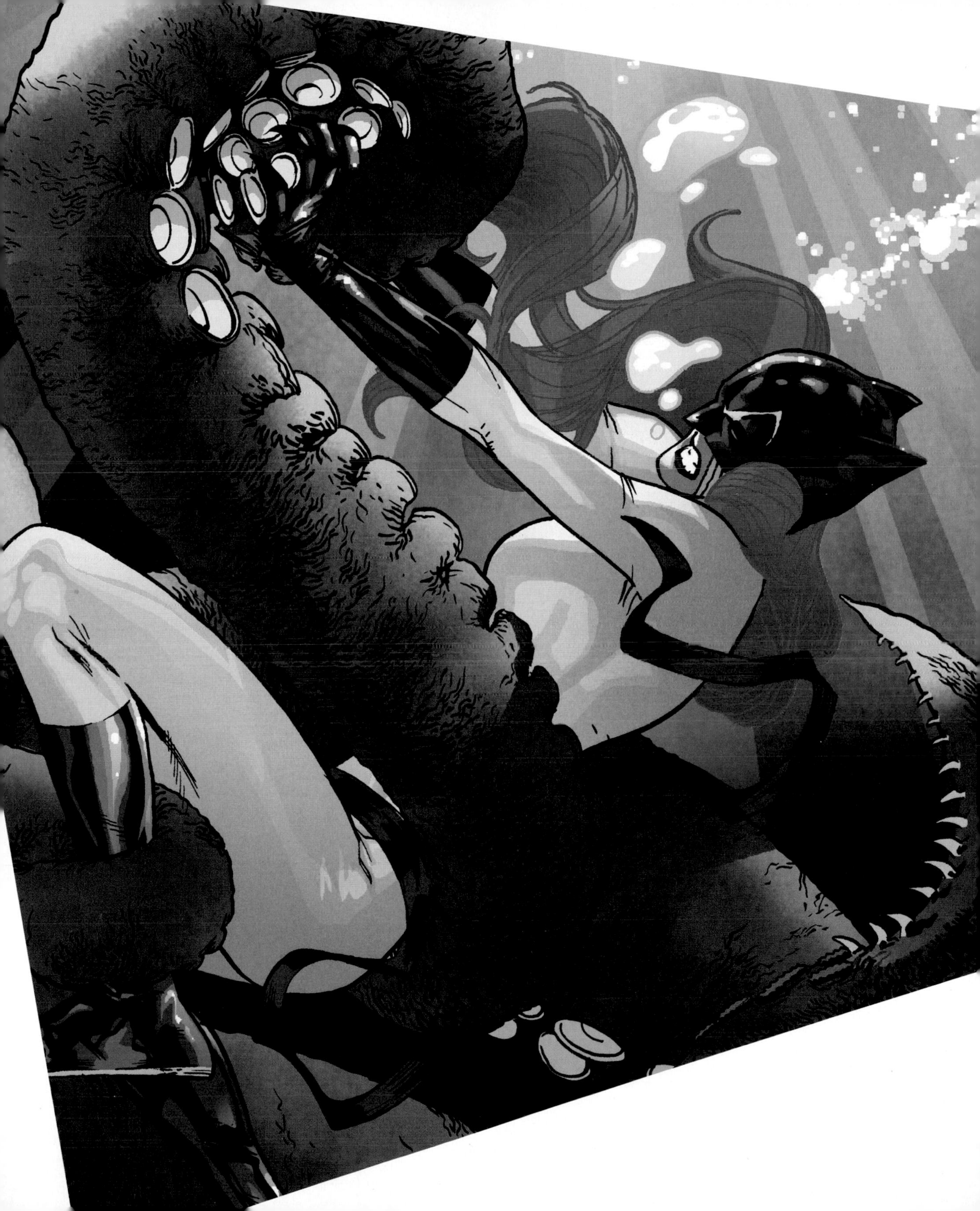

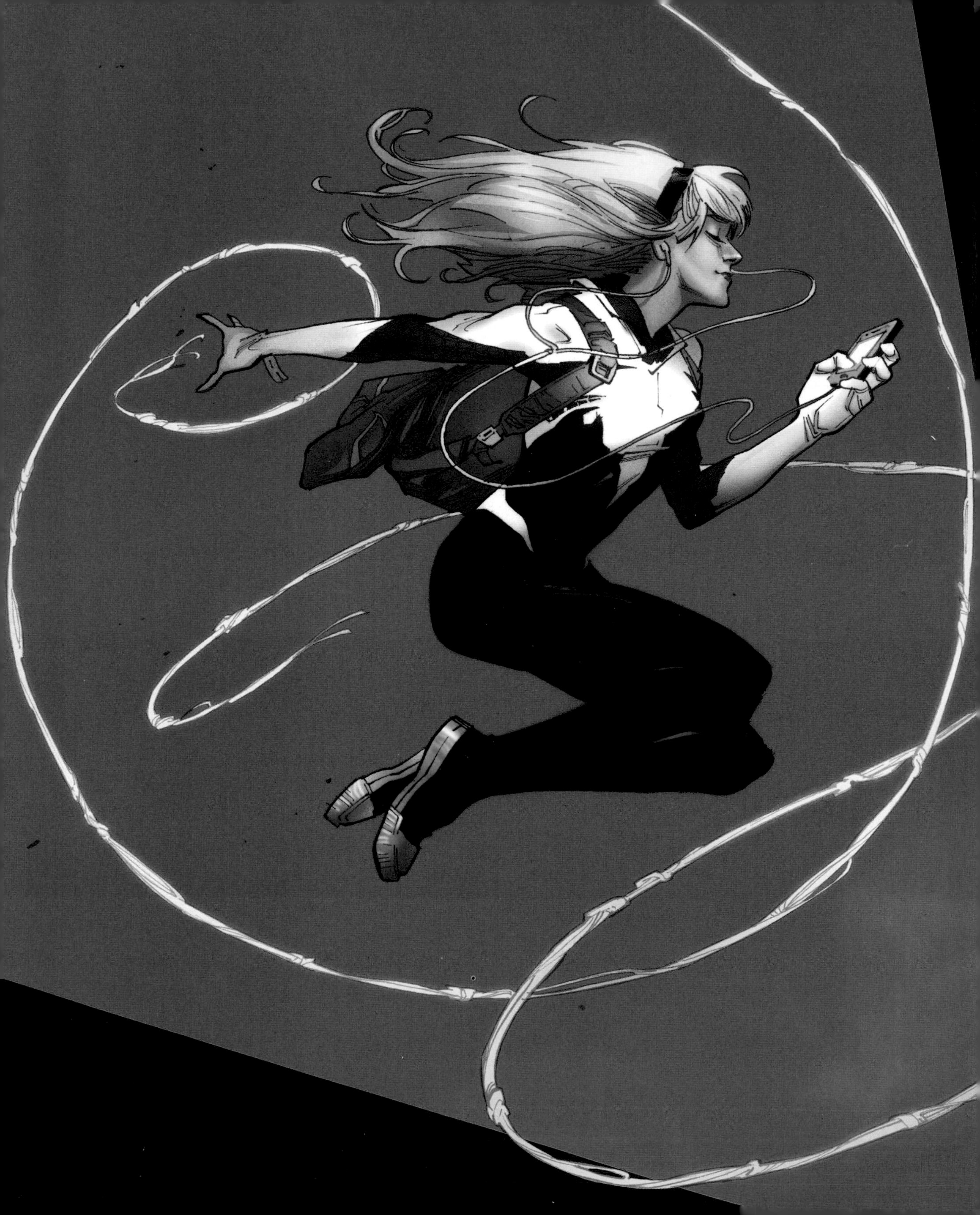

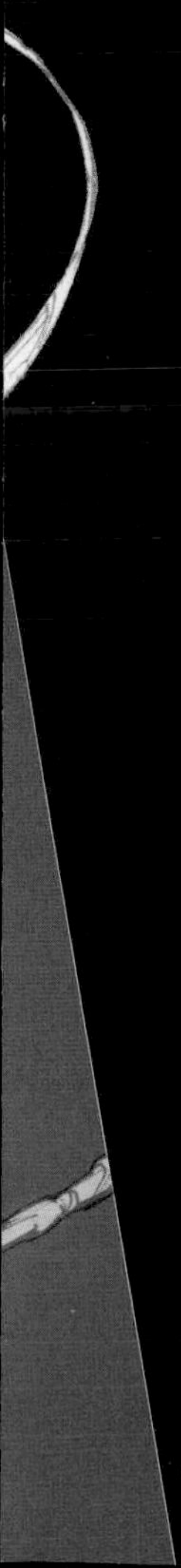

SPIDER-WOMAN

"You came looking for me? Well, here I am!
I'm not afraid of you!"

In an alternate universe, a radioactive spider bit teenager Gwen Stacy instead of Peter Parker. Gwen gained many powers, including super-speed, sticky fingertips and toes that helped her to climb up walls, and a sharpened sense of when danger was near. At first, Gwen used her powers for her own benefit, though she soon vowed to use them to help others. Gwen takes on criminals in New York City, but is branded the outlaw "Spider-Woman" by local newspapers. Life can be tricky for Gwen—her father, Captain George Stacy, works for the police force, which is investigating Spider-Woman's so-called crimes.

Witty Gwen can talk her way out of captivity easily. She uses web-shooters to swoop through the city, and has a transporter watch that creates portals for traveling to other realities. She has fought foes including Vulture and the Sinister Six, and has joined the brave Web-Warriors—a team of Spider-Women and Men from many different universes. Music-mad Gwen plays the drums in an awesome rock band known as "The Mary Janes," but her adventures mean she is often late to band practice and gigs.

Friends, allies, and role models:
Silk (p32), **Spider-Woman—Jessica Drew** (p102), **Spider-Girl** (p120)

MARIA HILL

"If I have something to answer for, I want to face it. If I can make good, I will."

Maria Hill is a dedicated member of defense organization S.H.I.E.L.D., having worked her way up through the ranks to serve in the agency's two most prestigious positions. Born in Chicago and trained as a Marine, Maria has no superhuman powers. Instead, she relies on her strong personality, espionage experience, and handgun proficiency to get the job done. When former leader Nick Fury left S.H.I.E.L.D., Maria was appointed director. She's tough and believes strongly in the chain of command—but she's been known to disobey immoral or otherwise suspicious orders when necessary.

After the infamous Civil War (in which people with powers battled over whether or not they should be forced to operate under strict government supervision), Maria stepped down as S.H.I.E.L.D.'s director, passing that role to Avenger Tony Stark. Though she has faced challenges in her career path since, Maria will likely always be a devoted agent of S.H.I.E.L.D. In her very limited downtime, she enjoys pizza and fantasy football.

Friends, allies, and role models:
Jessica Jones (p34), **Quake** (p64), **Pepper Potts** (p90)

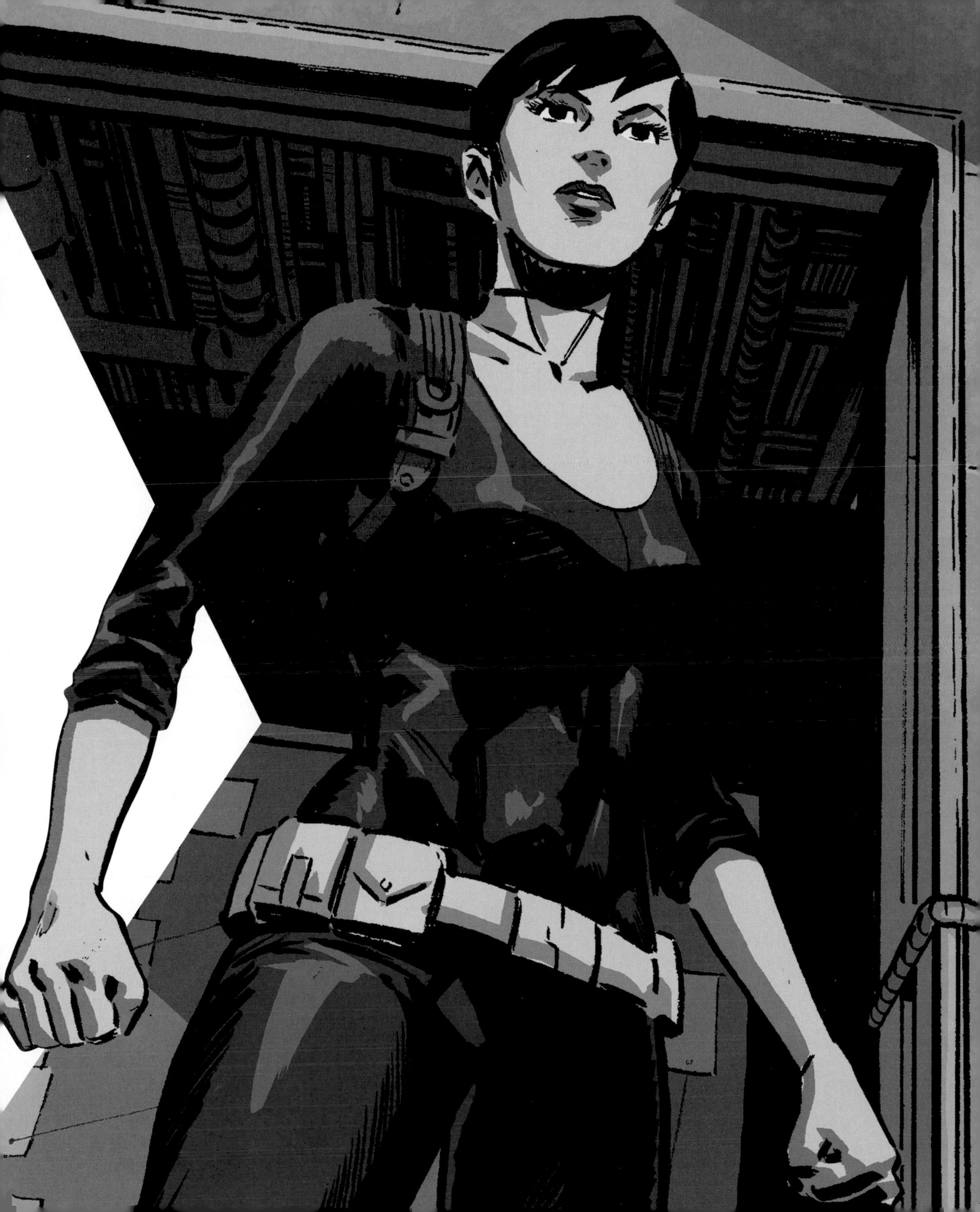

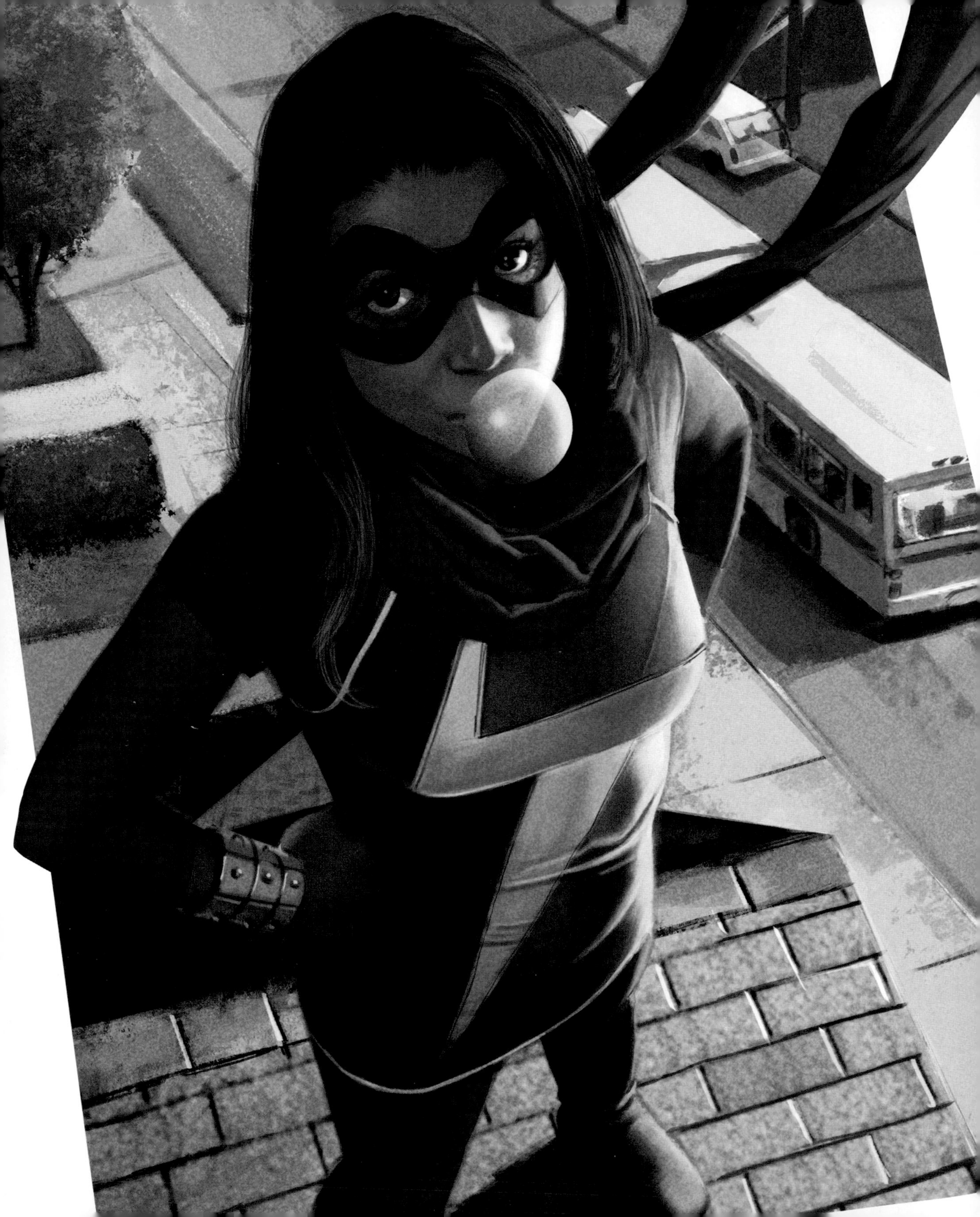

MS. MARVEL

"Help us win the hard way—the right way—
not with hate, not with retribution,
but with wisdom and hope."

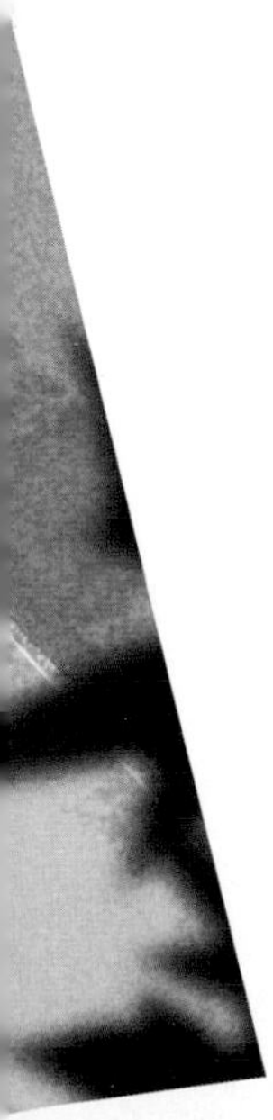

Kamala Khan was just a typical 16-year-old Pakistani-American Muslim girl in New Jersey, trying to balance family expectations, maintain good grades, and play *World of Battlecraft*. Exposed to Terrigen Mists while she was sneaking out one night, Kamala's hitherto-unknown Inhuman powers were activated, and she suddenly found herself in the form of her idol Carol Danvers (originally known as Ms. Marvel). Once Kamala gained control of her powers she discovered she was a polymorph with healing skills, able to mold her body shape into anything, and shrink or enlarge herself at will.

Self-titled nerd Kamala never questioned whether she should use her powers for good. Taking on the name "Ms. Marvel" and wearing a costume inspired by the traditional shalwar kameez garment, Kamala started chasing crooks in Jersey City. Her success on the battlefield, even when scared (of injury or, worse, parental punishment) gained the attention of the Avengers. She now works with the young Champions team and writes Super Hero fan fiction in her spare time.

Friends, allies, and role models:
Captain Marvel (p12), **Wasp—Nadia Van Dyne** (p108), **Moon Girl** (p110)

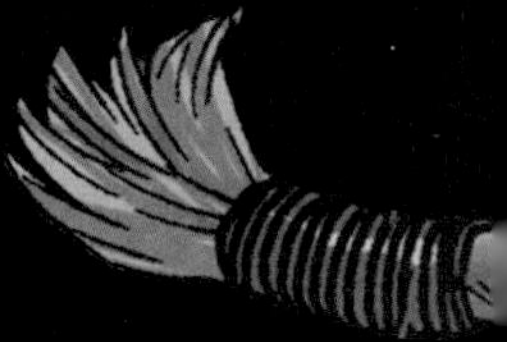

VALKYRIE

"The Valkyrie needs not help from you or any other man."

Born in the realm of Asgard, Brunnhilde began warrior training as a child alongside her friend Sif and god of thunder, Thor. She was chosen to head up the all-female Valkyrior group—responsible for leading worthy mortals who died in battle to Valhalla, the Asgardian afterlife. Valkyrie, as Brunnhilde became known, has the superior physical abilities common to all Asgardians, but her strength, stamina, and agility are enhanced by countless years of combat. She can also sense oncoming danger. Valkyrie's favorite weapons are her enchanted spear and her indestructible sword, Dragonfang.

Valkyrie sympathizes with humans, and her time spent with the Secret Avengers and Defenders teams earned her the nickname "The Defender of Earth." She briefly set up a new Valkyrior on Earth, named the Fearless Defenders—an all-female team that included Misty Knight. One of Valkyrie's great loves was a human archaeologist, Annabelle Riggs, who stopped Valkyrie from transforming into an evil member of the Doom Maidens. Valkyrie can often be seen fighting on the back of her winged horse, Aragorn.

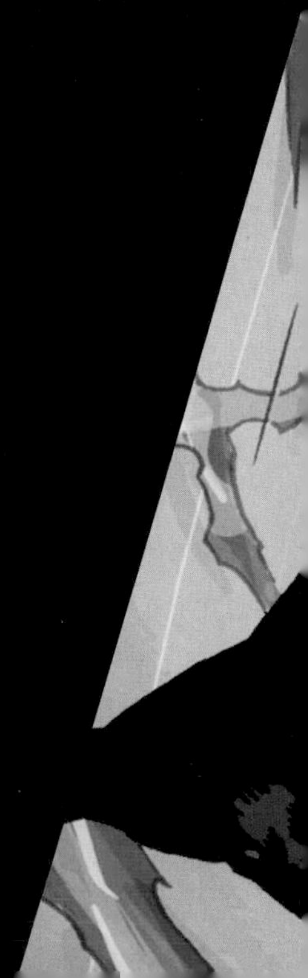

Friends, allies, and role models:
Sif (p14), **Thor—Jane Foster** (p50), **Misty Knight** (p60)

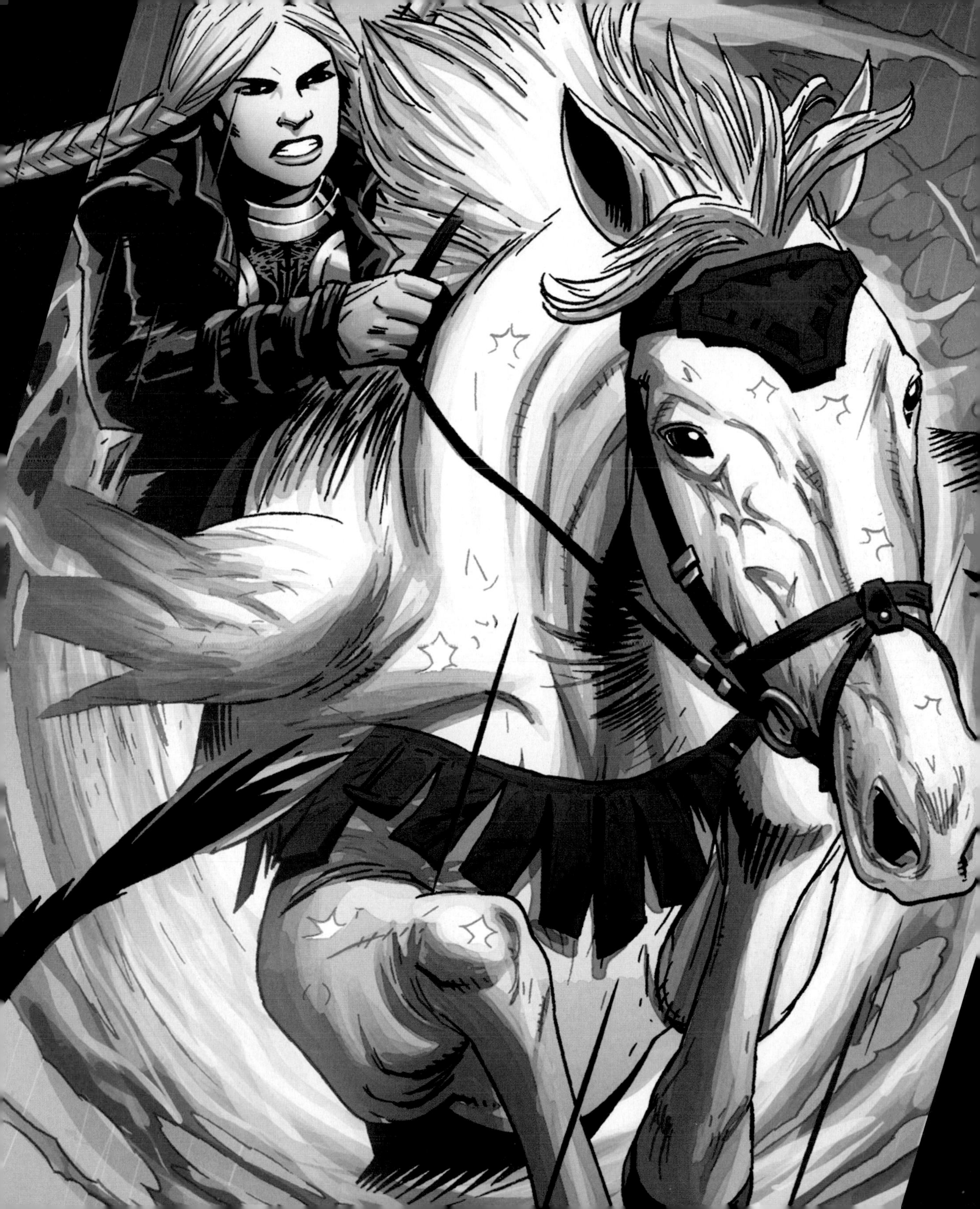

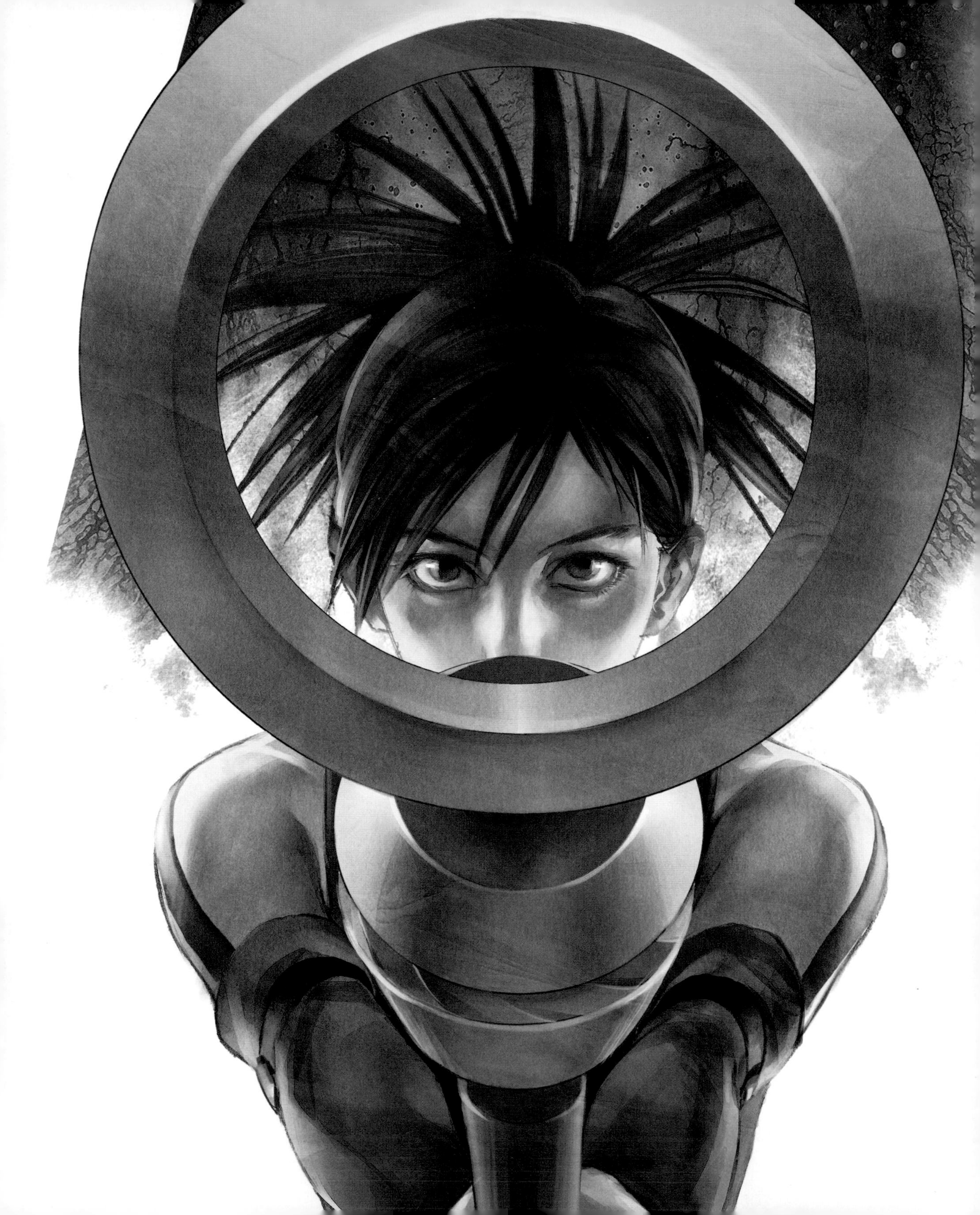

NICO MINORU

"That's the one thing we can't hide, huh?
Our roots."

Nico Minoru was just 16 when she discovered her Japanese-American parents were dark sorcerers and part of an organization of Super Villains named the Pride. She ran away from home with a group of other children of Pride members, creating their own, new family they dubbed "the Runaways." Like her parents, Nico is a witch, although, without proper training, she has trouble knowing the full extent of her powers. What she does know is she can call forth the magical Staff of One from her chest. With the Staff in hand, Nico can say any word to invoke a spell—the trick being that she can only use each word once, and never again. The Staff hates duplication.

Nico became leader of the Runaways and briefly went by the code name "Sister Grimm," which was her instant messenging screen name and a nod to her love of dark, goth clothing (much of which she makes herself). Nico has learned the word for "heal" in every language that she can, since it's a spell she has to use frequently, and this loophole bypasses the Staff's restrictions. She has complicated feelings for her teammate Karolina, and her catchphrase is "Try not to die."

Friends, allies, and role models:
Gertrude Yorkes (p38), **Karolina Dean** (p96), **Molly Hayes** (p122)

SILK

"My personal life? Not strong. But I did beat up a Hydra tentacle-monster-robot-thingie. So I got that going for me."

Korean-American student Cindy Moon was bitten by the same radioactive spider that bit fellow student Peter Parker and caused him to become the web-slinging hero Spider-Man. Cindy was already naturally gifted with a photographic memory, but after being bitten she gained spiderlike abilities similar to Peter's: heightened senses, wall-crawling, and amazing speed and agility. Pursued by a villain named Morlun hunting all those with spider-powers, Cindy hid in a bunker to protect herself and her family.

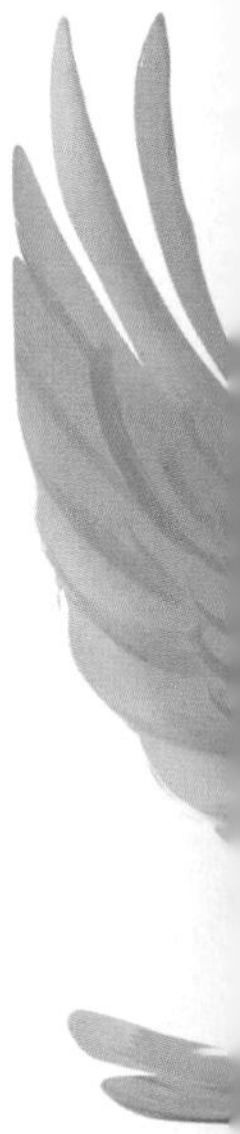

Years later, with Morlun defeated, Cindy took on the moniker "Silk" and began fighting evil alongside Spider-Man. Silk's speed, agility, and Spider-Senses (or "Silk-Senses") are superior to other spider-heroes', and she has the unique ability to generate organic silk webbing from her fingertips. After her period of isolation, Cindy's driving force was to find her parents and reclaim her past (and to catch up on pop culture). Briefly a Fact Channel News journalist, Silk is now in S.H.I.E.L.D. Academy training to become a future agent.

Friends, allies, and role models:

Gwen Stacy (p22), **Mockingbird** (p72), **Jessica Drew** (p102)

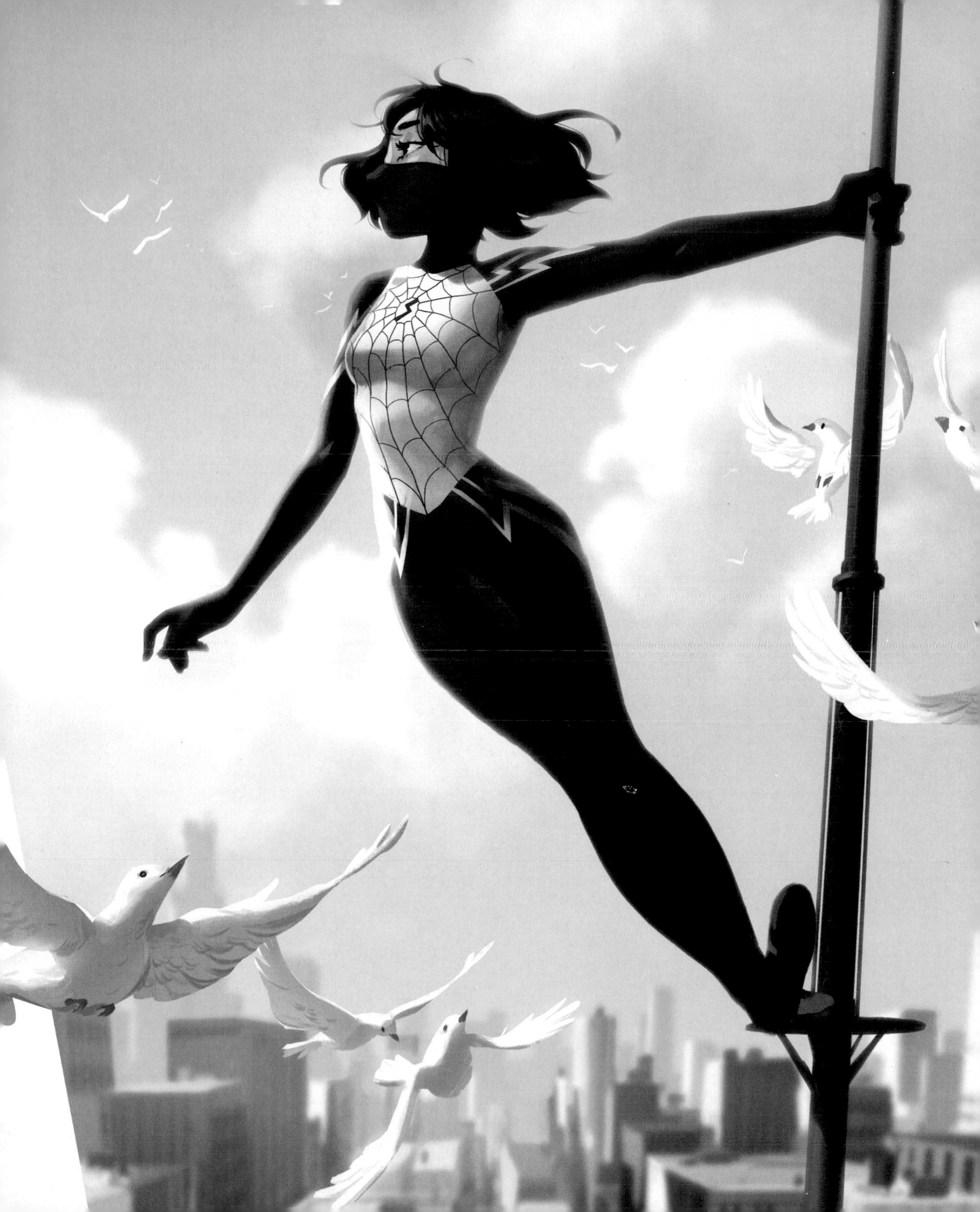

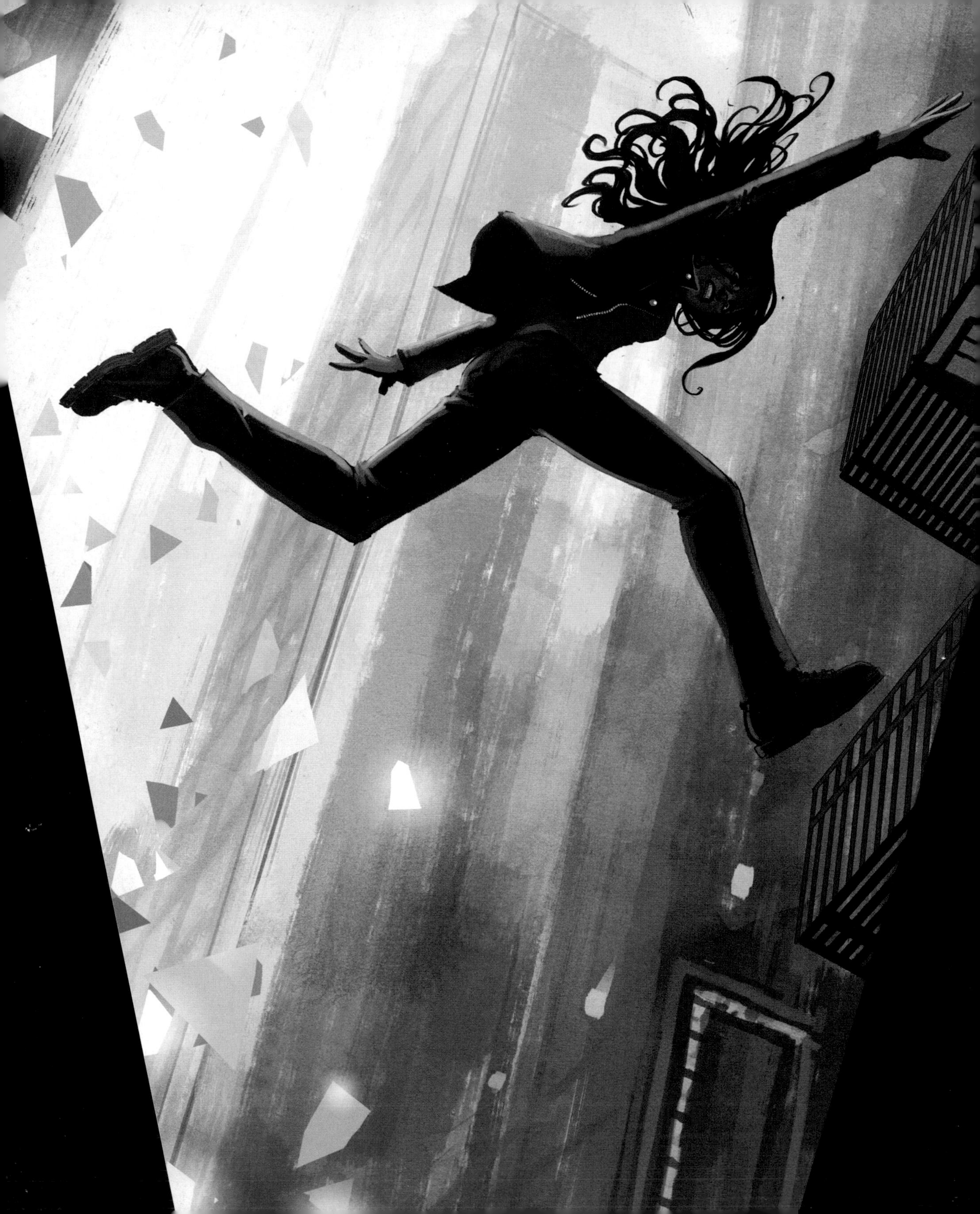

JESSICA JONES

"I am **very good** at **finding people.** Is there someone else I can help **you** find? Maybe the person that did **that** to your **hair?"**

Jessica Campbell Jones wasn't always New York City's greatest private investigator. She started her career as a Super Hero named Jewel after being accidentally exposed to radiation as a child—gaining super-strength, durability, and the power of flight. Jewel was captured and held prisoner by the mind-controlling Purple Man for months. After her escape, Jessica opened her own detective agency, Alias Investigations, to help the people of the city on a more personal level and to help her cope with her own difficult past. Jessica's first client was Luke Cage, her future husband.

Jessica is street-smart and sarcastic but secretly bighearted. She takes her duties as a private investigator very seriously, finding and rescuing young women in need of aid. She has recently defeated her old enemy, the Purple Man. Jessica has also worked with the *Daily Bugle* newspaper, the Avengers, and the Defenders. She and Luke have one daughter named Danielle, and in the past they have employed Squirrel Girl as her babysitter.

Friends, allies, and role models:
Captain Marvel (p12), **Misty Knight** (p60), **Echo** (p112)

QUEEN RAMONDA

"I take no joy in doing my duty, **but I will do it, even as others falter.**"

Queen Mother Ramonda is the quiet but forceful presence behind the throne of Wakanda and its king, T'Challa—otherwise known as the Black Panther. Ramonda was second wife to the previous king, T'Chaka, and mother to Princess Shuri. She has resolutely faced protests: as a South African and not a Wakandan, she was a controversial choice for queen. However, decades later, she has become a respected matriarch and is often sought out for her wise advice.

As Queen Mother, Ramonda oversees the *Dora Milaje*, the all-female bodyguards that protect Wakanda. She also settles disputes between all 18 tribes of Wakanda to ensure the laws of the nation are upheld. This often means making difficult decisions, such as having to pass a death sentence against *Dora Milaje* Captain Aneka, convicted of killing a chieftain. Ramonda regrets having to do so, but knows that as a fair judge she cannot allow her feelings to get in the way of the law. In her many years of service, Ramonda has seen the great advances Wakandans have made. She remains the bridge between all things new and traditional.

Friends, allies, and role models:
Storm (p16), **Ayo** (p74), **Shuri** (p100)

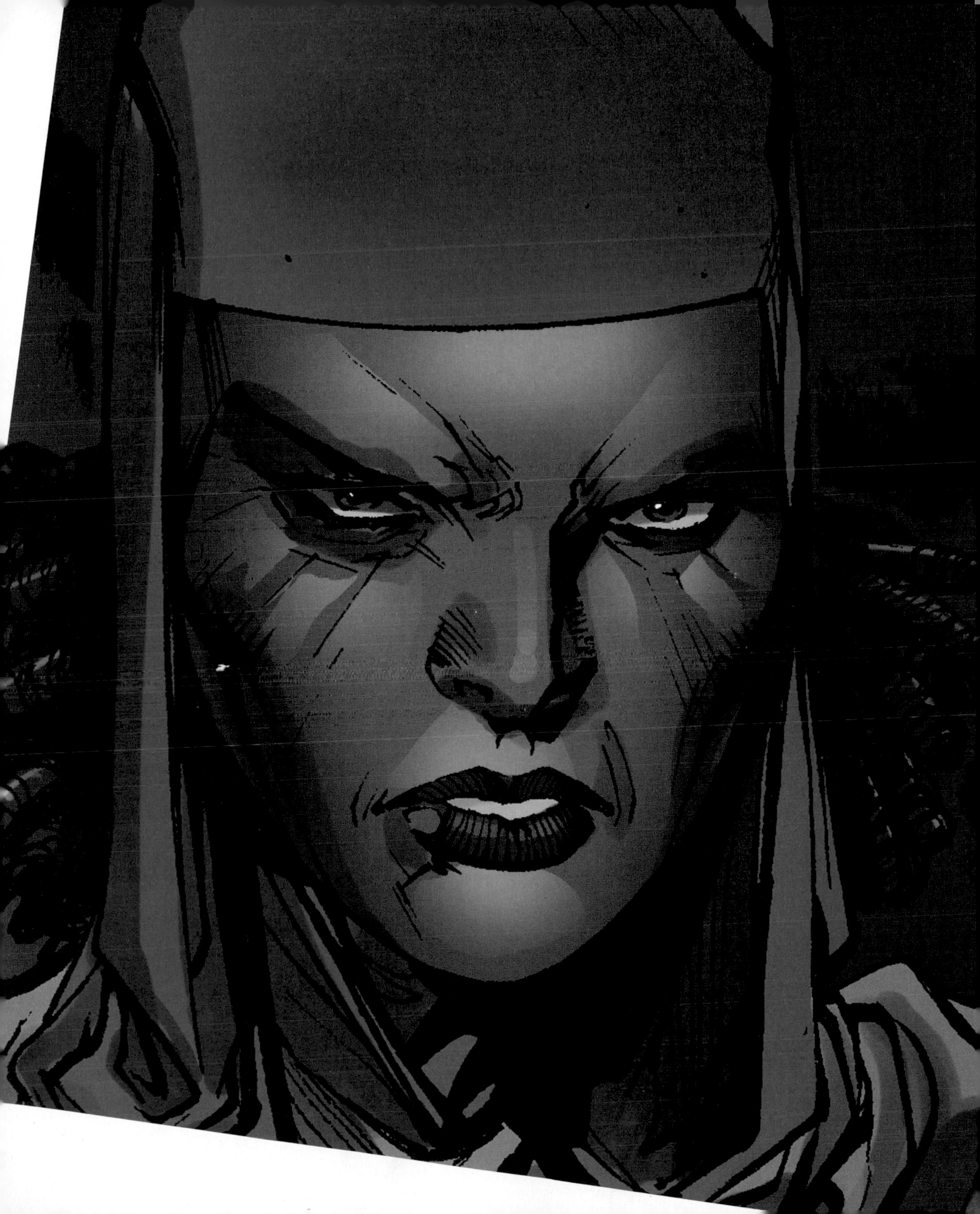

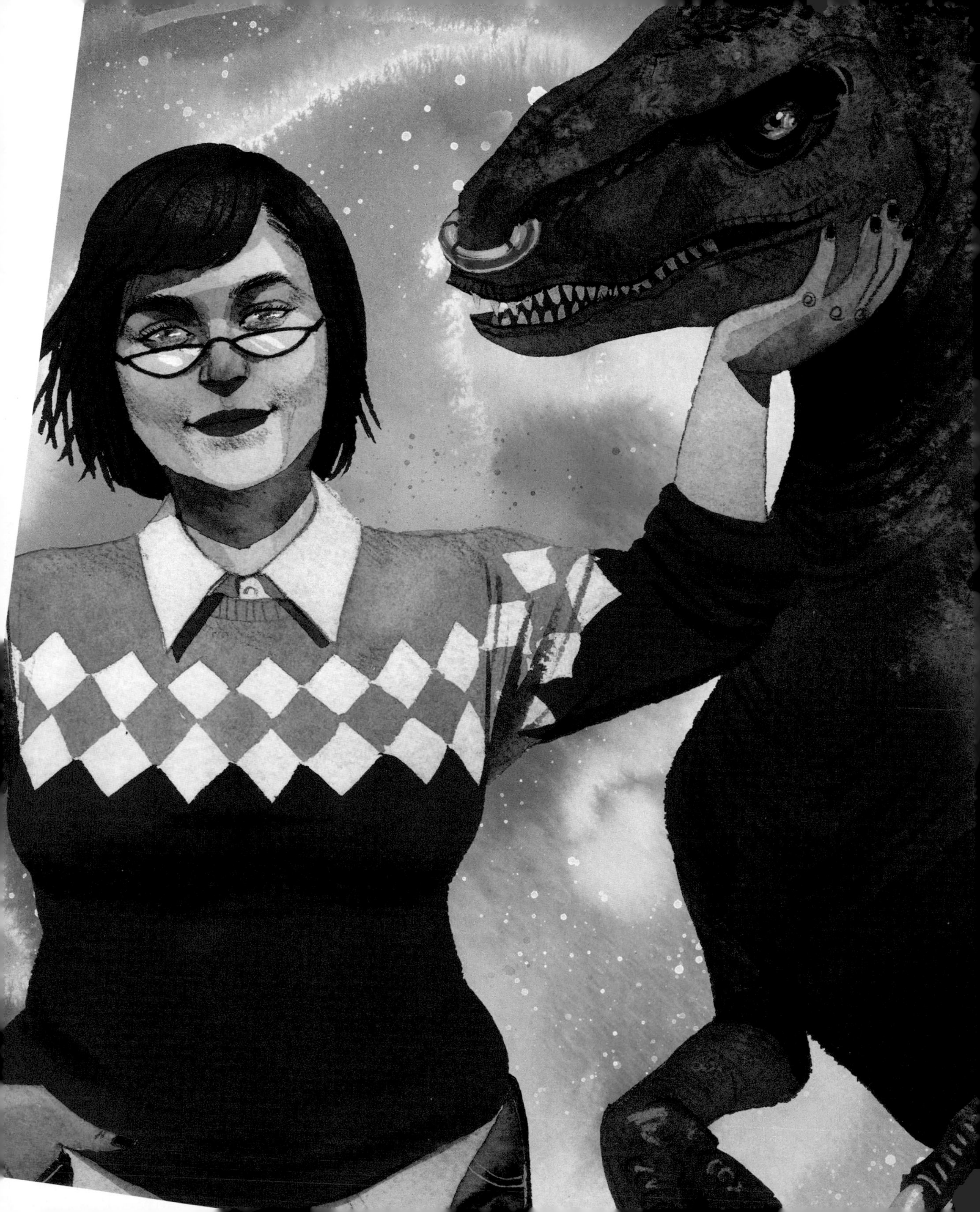

GERTRUDE YORKES

"I've got a perfectly fine head. And I've got a more-than-fine brain."

A slightly clumsily executed time-traveling trick has brought gutsy Gertrude "Gert" Yorkes back from what seemed like certain death. Determined to reunite her Runaways teammates, Gert is also trying to reconcile her past self with her present self. Her loyalty to her team is unswayed: with them she has fought mystical giant deities, the Avengers' archenemy Ultron, and even foster care!

Gert has no super-powers, but she makes up for it with a fast wit, smart brains, and a telepathic link with a genetically created *Deinonychus* (a carnivorous dinosaur) she named Old Lace. Her parents may have been merely human, but they were time-travelers from the future, and it was they who brought back the dinosaur from the 87th century, designed to obey Gert's every command. Of all the Runaways, Gert was the only one not surprised to discover that their collective parents were in fact evil villains in a group called the Pride. She temporarily took the name "Arsenic" in order to cut all ties with them. Gert remains distrustful of all adults.

Friends, allies, and role models:
Nico Minoru (p30), **Karolina Dean** (p96), **Molly Hayes** (p122)

JUBILEE

"We can do anything. We can be anyone. That's the definition of being alive. That's magic."

Generation X team leader Jubilation Lee is able to create fireworks at will, but discovered this skill by accident. Born to wealthy Chinese immigrants in Beverly Hills, Jubilee loved fashion and shopping. After her parents were killed by a criminal, Jubilee ran away to live in the only place she felt at home: the shopping mall. She found that she had mutant powers when she generated a massive flash while running from the mall's security guards. Rescued by the X-Men, she learned her "fireworks" were actually mind-controlled bursts of plasma energy.

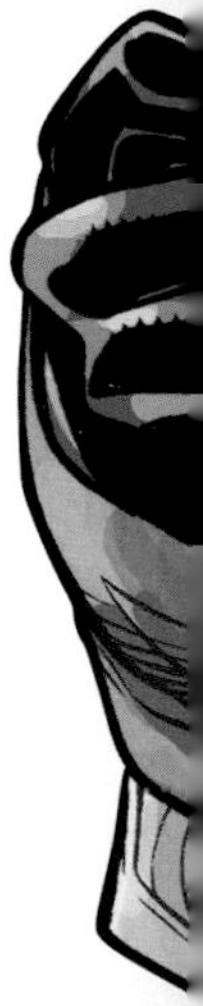

With training at the Xavier School for Gifted Youngsters, Jubilee became a powerful X-Men member herself. She also joined teen "neo-mutant" squad Generation X, which she now leads. She refuses to take anyone's life—even that of her parents' killer. For a time, she was infected with a virus that turned her into a vampire, but fortunately she has since been cured. Fun and impulsive, Jubilee loves skateboarding, gaming, her signature yellow coat, and above all, her adopted son, Shogo.

Friends, allies, and role models:
Hellcat (p20), **Jean Grey** (p86), **Kitty Pryde** (p116), **Dazzler** (p124)

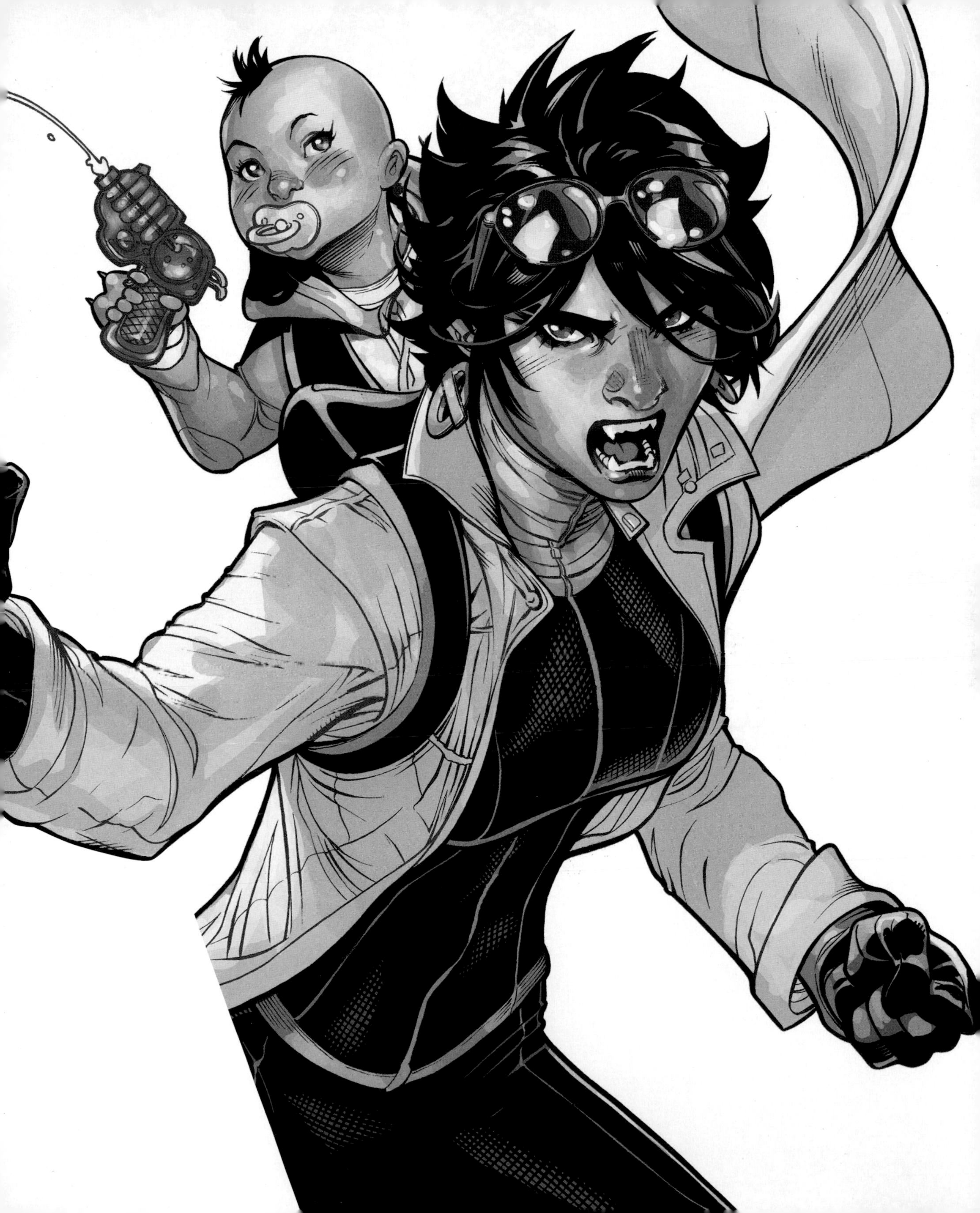

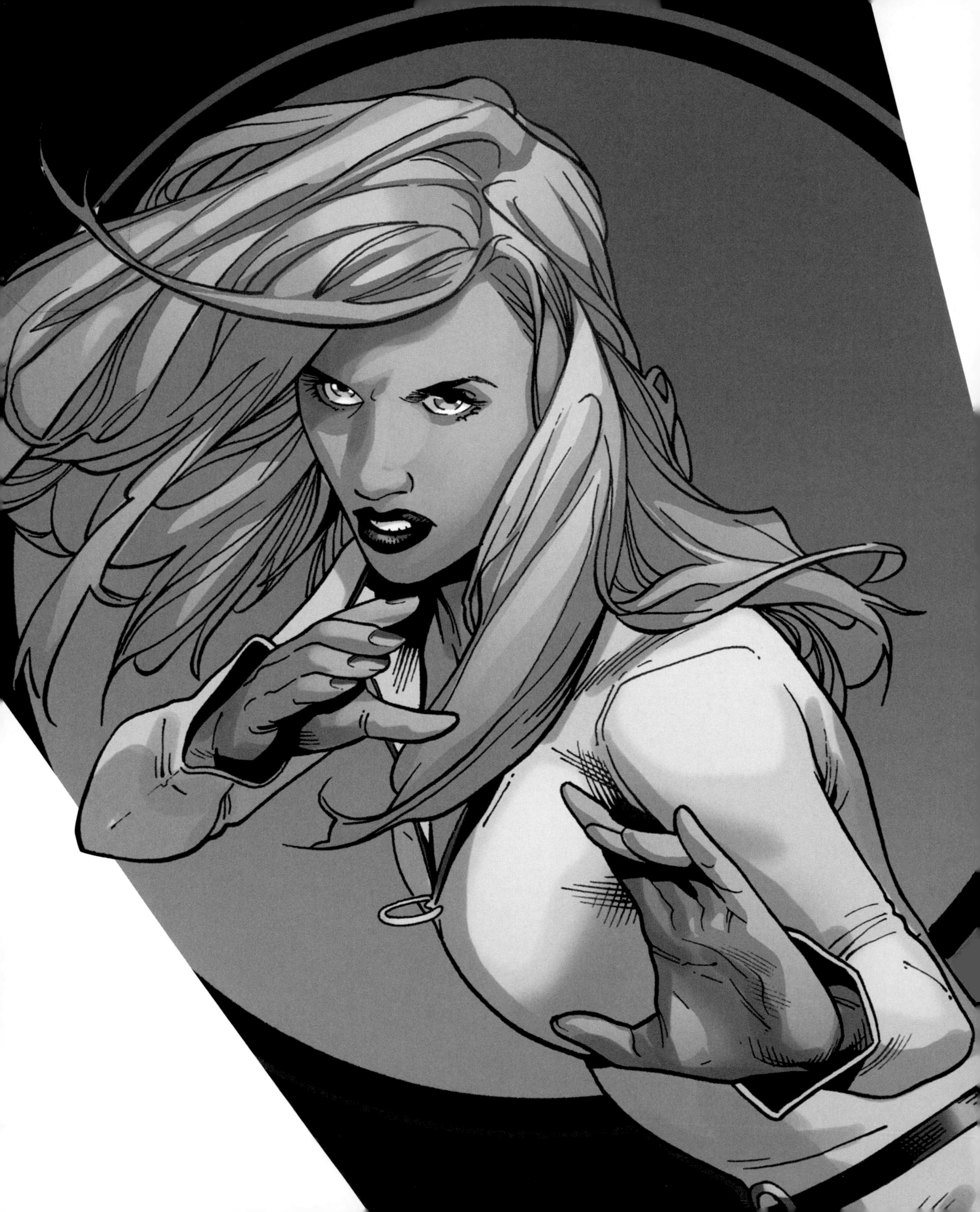

SHARON CARTER

"I'm not the kind of person to choose love over duty."

Sharon Carter grew up hearing stories of her brave aunt Peggy, who was a World War II resistance fighter and instrumental in the shaping of secret organization S.H.I.E.L.D. Inspired by her famous family member, Sharon joined S.H.I.E.L.D. and was assigned the code name "Agent 13." She received extensive training in espionage, hand-to-hand combat, and computer hacking. Sharon is a crack shot with a sniper rifle. She often fights alongside Captain America, countering his idealistic views with her more realistic outlook.

Sharon has defeated minions of evil Hydra and Red Skull, worked as the S.H.I.E.L.D. liaison to the New York Police Department to take down a villainous political organization, and founded S.H.I.E.L.D.'s short-lived commando squad Femme Force. She has been so successful within S.H.I.E.L.D. that she has served as director during the absences of leaders Nick Fury and Maria Hill. When Sharon isn't protecting Captain America and S.H.I.E.L.D. from the forces of evil, she is searching for the world's greatest hamburger.

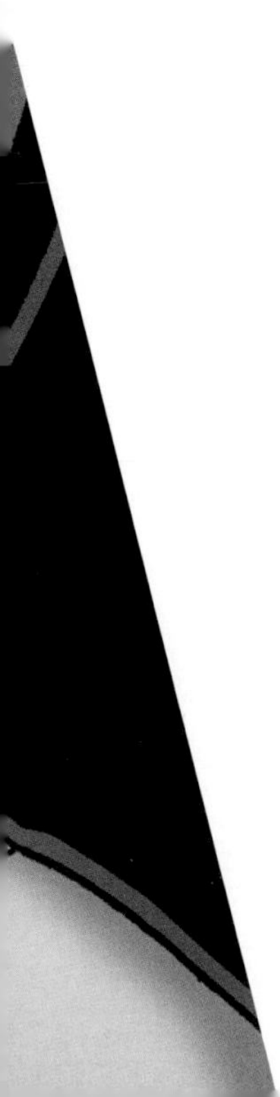

Friends, allies, and role models:
Black Widow (p18), **Maria Hill** (p24), **Peggy Carter** (p54)

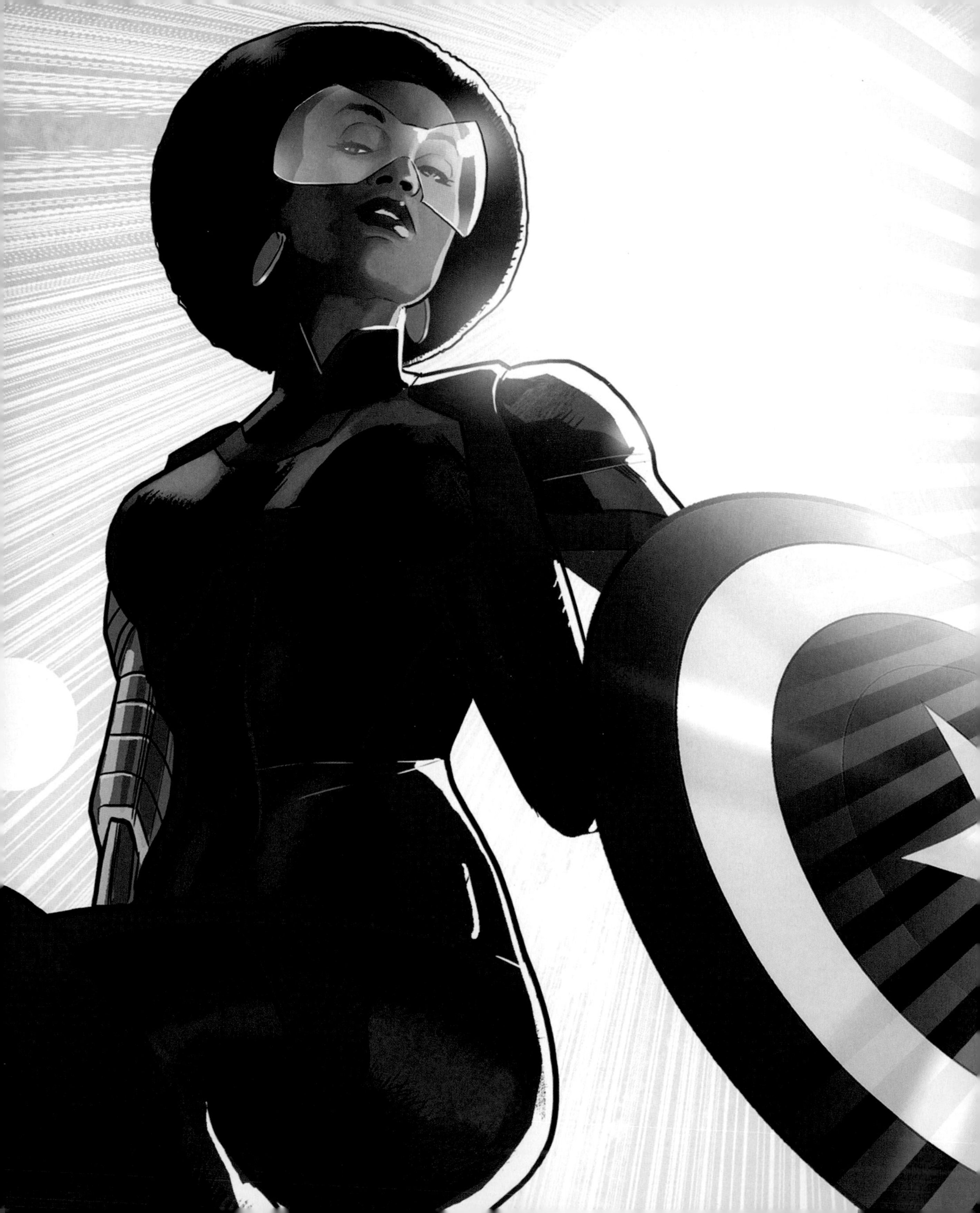

DARING

Risk-taking, bold, and fearless, these Super Heroes are always ready for adventure. From the streets of modern Manhattan to the depths of outer space, they overcome great odds and never shirk from danger. The courageous actions of Thor, Gamora, Hawkeye, and more have saved the world from peril time and time again.

◀ Misty Knight (p60)

WASP

"My secret power is that
I get things done."

An influential scientist's daughter, courageous Janet Van Dyne turned to the biochemist Hank Pym, aka Ant-Man, to avenge her father's death at the hands of an alien. Genetically modified by Hank's powerful Pym Particles, Janet discovered she could shrink to the size of a wasp and sprout silky wings. Janet's compressed body mass granted her superhuman strength, and her wings gave her the ability to fly at incredible speeds. She could also shoot powerful "stinger blasts" from her hands. With this combination of powers, Janet became the Wasp, taking down her father's killer and continuing to fight for justice.

Together with Ant-Man and the heroes Thor, Iron Man, and Hulk, Janet was a founding member of the Avengers, having suggested its name herself. Janet is a strong commander; she has led the Avengers on several occasions, and only Captain America has helmed the Super Hero team for longer than her. Outgoing, confident, and intelligent, Janet has never felt the need to use a secret identity. Janet is also a fashion designer and creates her own costumes.

Friends, allies, and role models:
Captain Marvel (p12), **She-Hulk** (p106), **Wasp—Nadia Van Dyne** (p108)

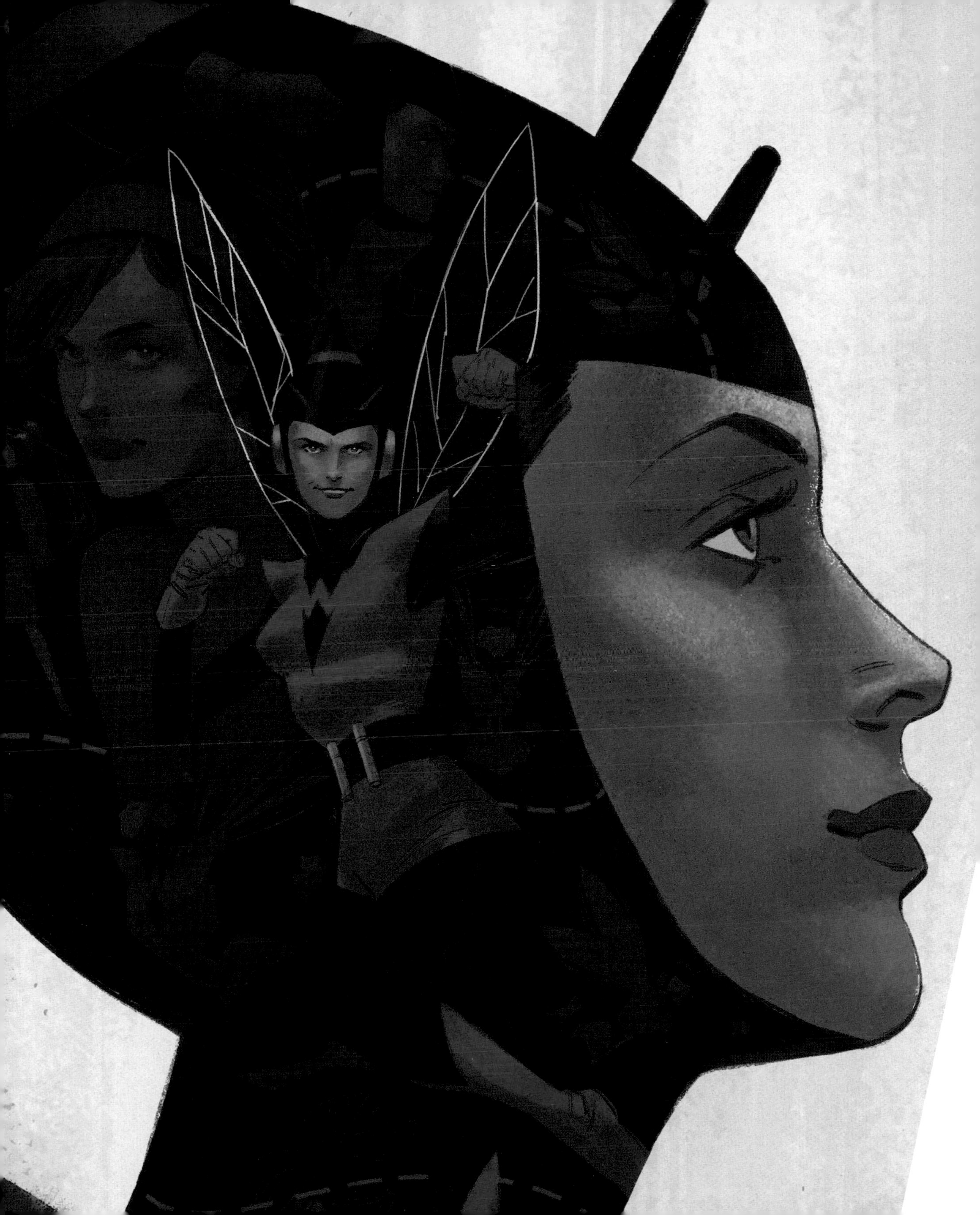

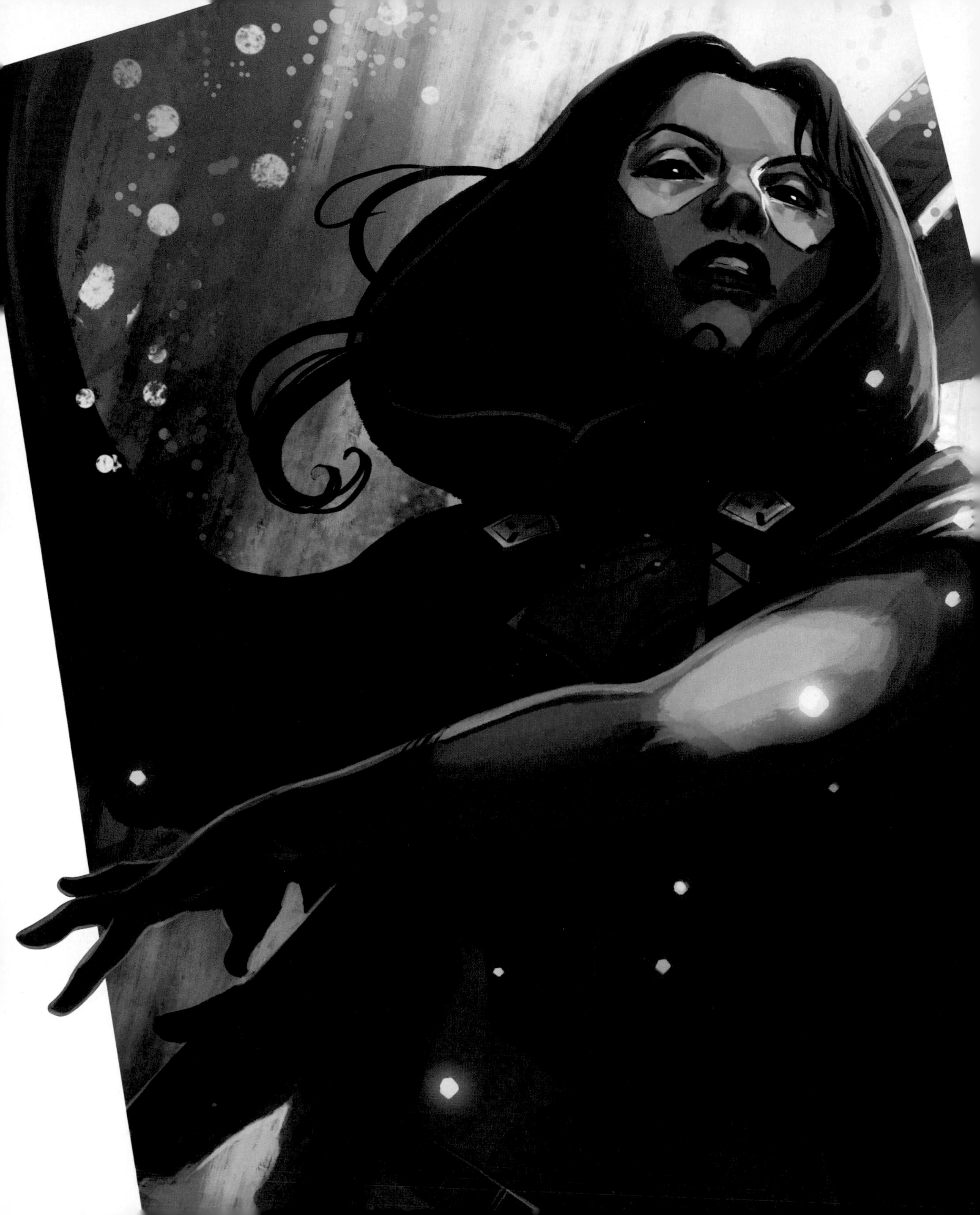

GAMORA

"I don't clean messes, I make them."

Gamora is an assassin skilled in most forms of armed and unarmed combat from different cultures across the galaxy (although her personal preference is swordfighting). The only surviving member of the Zen-Whoberi race, Gamora was "rescued" by the mad tyrant Thanos when she was just a child. Thanos raised Gamora to be a master of martial arts and self-discipline, while also enhancing her physically with bionic implants that increased her reflexes and strength. She can also heal rapidly, possesses unbreakable bones, and can even survive for short periods of time in the vacuum of space.

On discovering that Thanos planned to destroy the galaxy with the Infinity Gauntlet—a device made up of a series of immensely powerful gemstones—Gamora dedicated herself to defending the universe from her adoptive father's evil plans. Gamora joined the high-spirited Guardians of the Galaxy squad on a search to find her purpose in life. She now travels the universe protecting the powerless. As devastating with her sarcasm as she is with her sword, Gamora is known as the deadliest woman in the galaxy.

Friends, allies, and role models:
Captain Marvel (p12), **Mantis** (p84), **She-Hulk** (p106)

THOR

"I care not what you call me… Just be certain to inform your new cellmates t'was a woman who returned you to prison."

Doctor Jane Foster was thunder god Thor's greatest ally on Earth until he became unworthy of wielding his magical hammer, Mjolnir. Mjolnir then called out to Jane, who, despite battling breast cancer at the time, reached the hammer and lifted it, transforming into her own version of Thor. She gained the god's strength, vitality, and lightning powers and her control over Mjolnir was uniquely impressive.

Thor kept her true identity a secret from the world, while she battled the Minotaur, Malekith the Accursed, and the Destroyer alongside an army of female Super Heroes. She represented Earth in the Congress of Worlds on Asgard and served as a member of the Avengers. Tragically, Jane's cancer treatment was ineffective while in god form. She chose to transform into Thor one last time to try to save the city of Asgardia from the evil creature Mangog, chaining the monster to Mjolnir and throwing them both into the sun. Thankfully, Jane returned to Earth with the original Thor's assistance, where she is human and on the path to recovery.

Friends, allies, and role models:
Sif (p14), **Valkyrie** (p28), **Squirrel Girl** (p82)

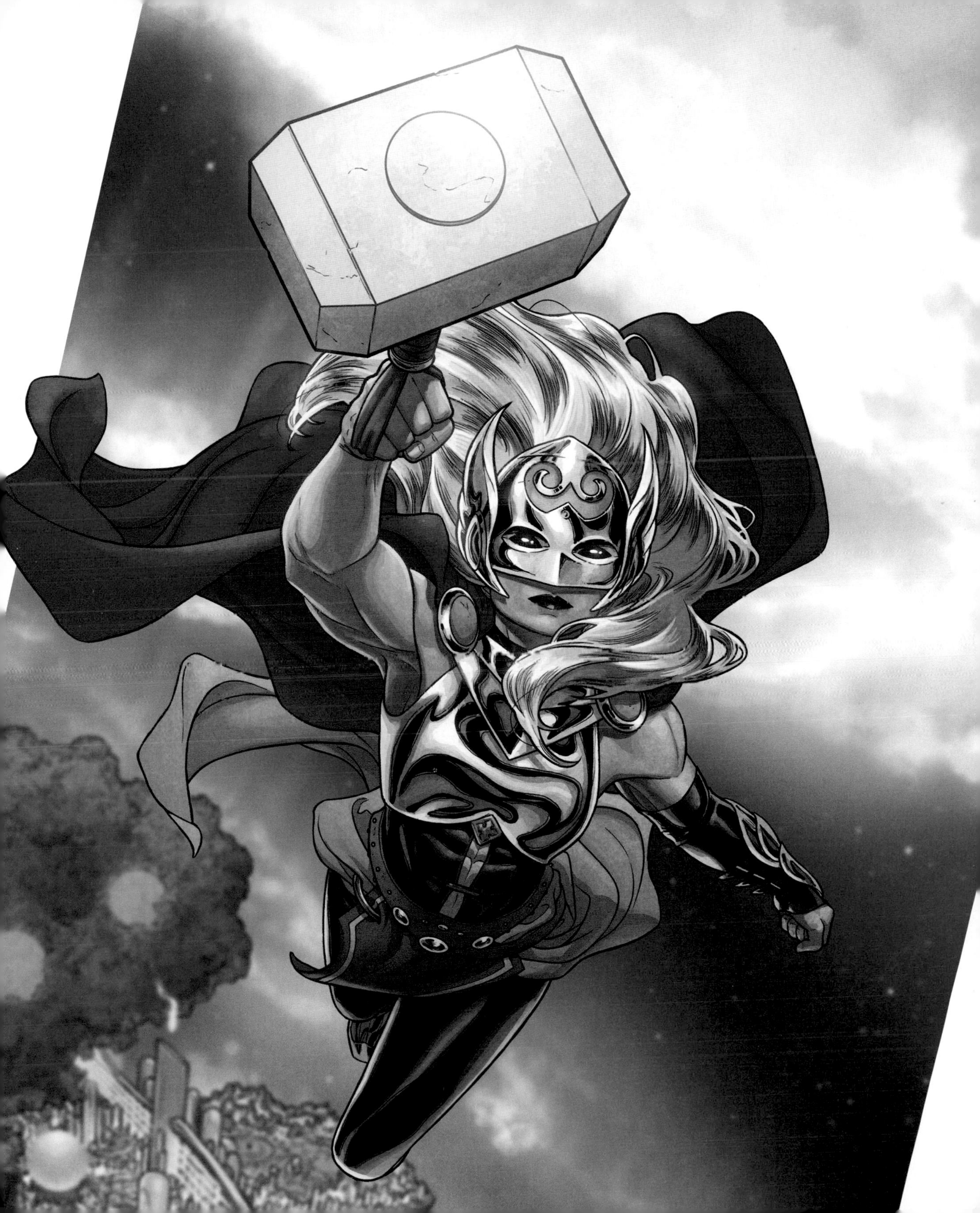

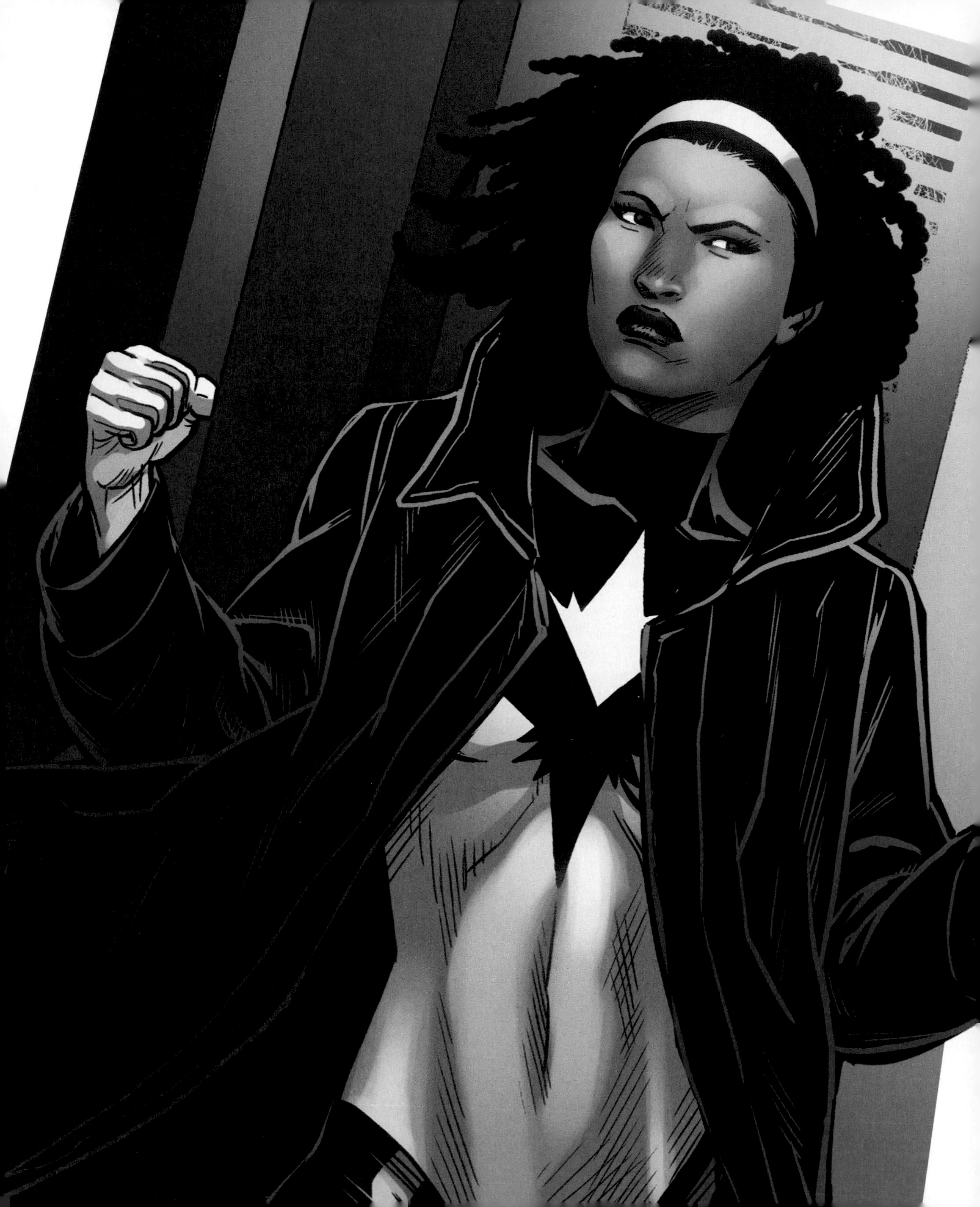

SPECTRUM

"We get back to work—for the people who need us. And if we have to, we do it all over again—only bigger."

New Orleans Harbor Patrol lieutenant Monica Rambeau was dedicated to protecting people before she even became a Super Hero. A run-in with an energy weapon created by a criminal scientist not only gave her super-powers, but also made her more determined than ever. After experimenting with her new abilities, Monica found she could phase through solid objects, transform her body into light or energy forms, move with superhuman speed, and become invisible. She sought out the Avengers for help and soon became a member of the team, trusted even to take on the mantle of Captain Marvel. Recognizing her leadership skills, Captain America nominated Monica to take over from him as team leader.

Later taking on her own unique alias, Spectrum—a nod to her energy powers—she teamed up with Luke Cage's Mighty Avengers team. On her mission to fight evil, she has even adventured into outer space. Spectrum has beaten injuries that should have floored her, and still finds time to travel back home to visit her parents—her first heroic role models.

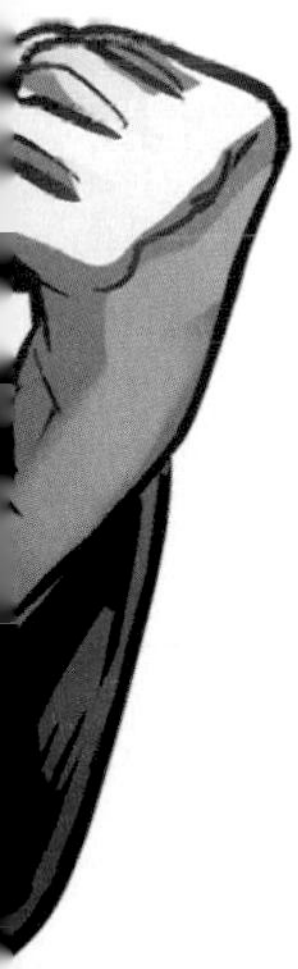

Friends, allies, and role models:
Captain Marvel (p12), **Hellcat** (p20), **Wasp—Janet Van Dyne** (p46)

PEGGY CARTER

"Lose battles but not wars? Lose heart but not hope? I am strong enough to do that..."

As a teenager, Margaret "Peggy" Carter joined the French Resistance to help overthrow the Nazis during World War II. She quickly became an expert detective and spy who rose in the ranks as a valued agent of the Resistance. For one of her missions, she was assigned to protect a secret laboratory hidden behind a false storefront—the lab where the Super-Soldier Serum transformed ordinary man Steve Rogers into the heroic Captain America. Peggy then fought together with Cap during the war to defeat many Nazi agents and members of Hydra, an evil international organization.

After working with the inventor Howard Stark in 1952 to stop Hydra from using dangerous alien technology in Siberia, Peggy joined the secret intelligence organization S.H.I.E.L.D. Taking the code name Agent 13, brave Peggy used her skills in marksmanship, spying, and close combat to hold S.H.I.E.L.D. to the high standards set by noble Cap in the 1940s. Peggy never took no for an answer, and paved the way for other women to become S.H.I.E.L.D. agents after her—such as her niece Sharon, the future Agent 13.

Friends, allies, and role models:
Sif (p14), **Sharon Carter** (p42), **Wasp—Janet Van Dyne** (p46)

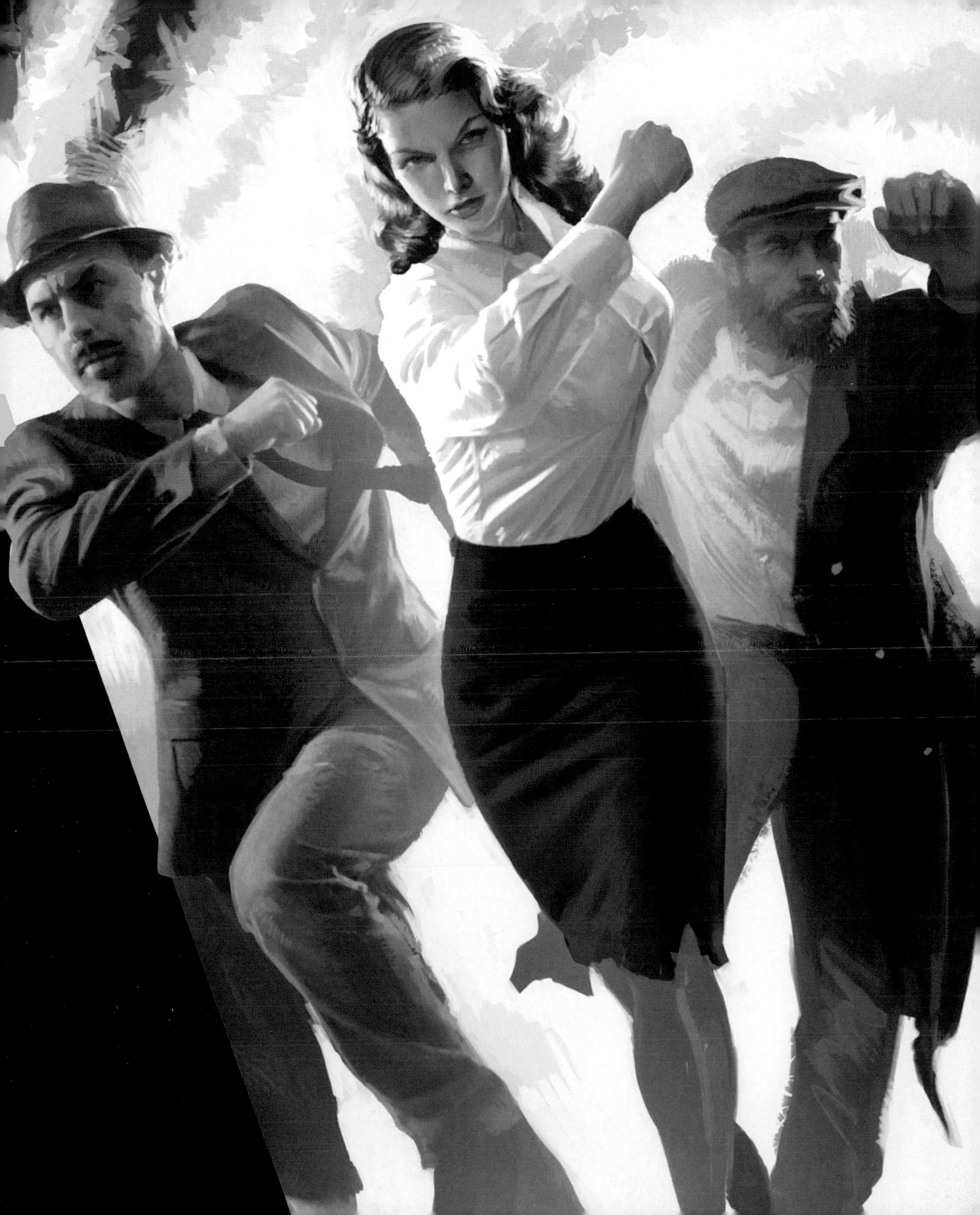

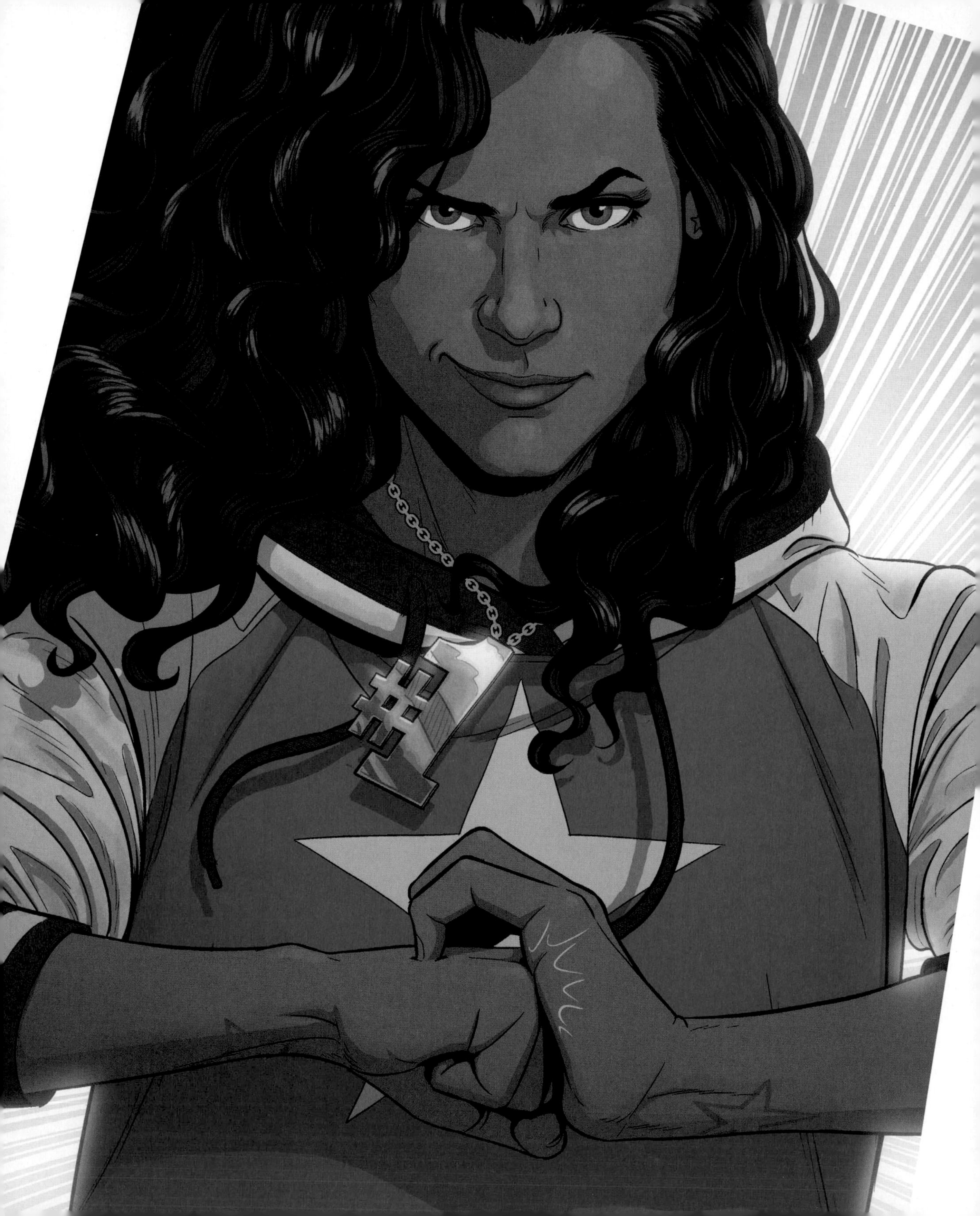

AMERICA CHAVEZ

"I want to be **better**, you know? Smarter. Stronger. **Just better.**"

Don't let her behavior fool you: America Chavez's tough exterior protects a warm heart. America was born in a paradise-like parallel universe populated entirely by women. She is capable of flight and of opening up star-shaped portals to other realities. She is also super-fast, super-strong, and entirely bulletproof. When their world was threatened, America's mothers Amalia and Elena sacrificed themselves to save it. In their honor, the fiercely independent America travels the Multiverse, seeking out those in need of protection.

Not a natural team player, America hops from team to team, universe to universe, protecting each alternate Earth mainly from interdimensional threats. In addition to her time with the Teen Brigade, Ultimates, Young Avengers, and West Coast Avengers teams, she has studied cultural history at the extradimensional Sotomayor University. America is fluent in both Spanish and English, and during her many travels she has found herself most accepted and comfortable in our Earth's Latin American communities, identifying as both Latinx and gay. She packs a mighty punch.

Friends, allies, and role models:
Storm (p16), **Spectrum** (p52), **Hawkeye** (p58)

HAWKEYE

"I have no powers and not nearly enough training, but I'm doing this anyways. Being a Super Hero is amazing. Everyone should try it."

Clever, blunt, and confident, Kate Bishop is remarkably devoted to helping those who need it most. She has put her vast family fortune to good use, donating to women's shelters and centers that provide free food. She studied at an elite private school, where she mastered archery, fencing, jujitsu, and kickboxing in order to protect herself and others. Inspired by Clint Barton, a member of the Avengers team with no super-powers, Kate used her skills and resources to become a key member of the Young Avengers.

Kate supplied the Young Avengers with outfits, gear, and even a fully-upgraded headquarters. Impressed by her dedication to the next generation of Super Heroes, Captain America sent Kate one of Clint's old bows—and permission to use Clint's old code name, "Hawkeye." Most recently, Kate traveled to LA, opening her own private investigation/Super Hero business to prove her independence. Her closest ally, America Chavez, calls Kate "Princess," much to her annoyance.

Friends, allies, and role models:
Hellcat (p20), **Jessica Jones** (p34), **America Chavez** (p56)

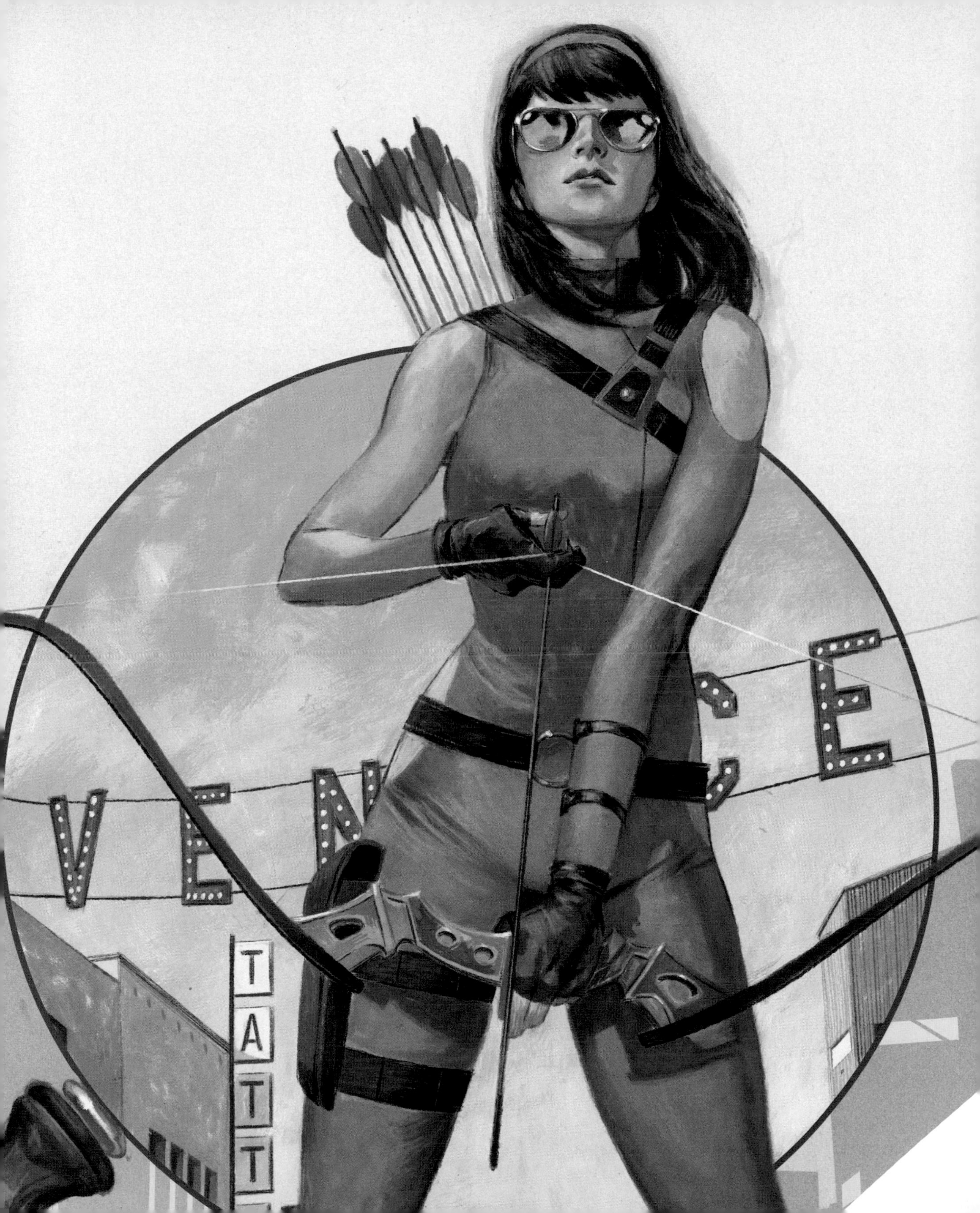
VEN
CE
TATT

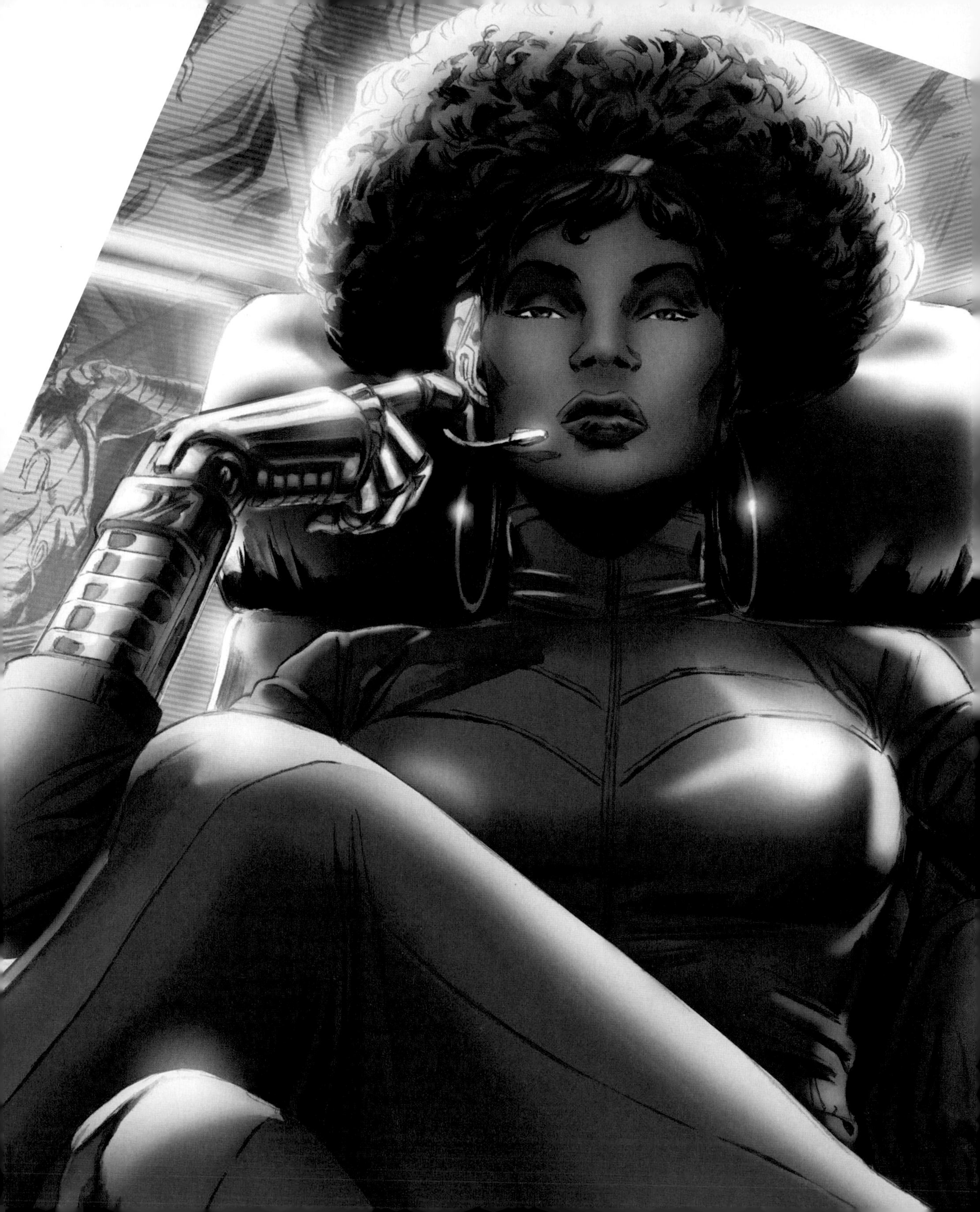

MISTY KNIGHT

"Come on, **heroes.** We've got to help **save** this city."

A brilliant martial artist and markswoman, Mercedes "Misty" Knight was born and raised in New York City. While working as an officer of the NYPD (New York Police Department), she was severely injured in the line of duty when a bomb exploded, losing her right arm. Her good friend and fellow martial artist Colleen Wing helped Misty through her recovery, and engineer Tony Stark provided Misty with a state-of-the-art, steel bionic arm as thanks for her service.

Leaving her job at the NYPD, Misty started a private investigation firm, Knightwing Restorations Ltd., alongside Colleen. Misty has worked closely with the Defenders, Heroes for Hire, and Valkyrie's Fearless Defenders groups, taking down the villains of the Hand ninja squad, crime bosses, and other forces that threaten her city. Misty's newest bionic arm is made from Vibranium metal. It is able to generate magnetic fields, ice beams, and stunning blasts, and can even control other technology. Her NYPD training has made her a talented detective, and her foes do not enjoy having to face her in the interrogation room. Misty does not take disrespect lightly.

Friends, allies, and role models:
Valkyrie (p28), **Colleen Wing** (p68), **Jean Grey** (p86)

MARY JANE WATSON

"Danger is my middle name.
I have it monogrammed on all of my towels."

Mary Jane "MJ" Watson grew up with fellow students Peter Parker and Gwen Stacy, discovering Peter's secret identity as the hero Spider-Man very early on. She has served as an invaluable support system for Peter, with whom she's had an on-again, off-again relationship over the years. MJ is a kind-hearted and loving person who cares deeply for Peter, but she prioritizes her own wellbeing and career over a relationship with a Super Hero and all its inevitable complications.

An accomplished model, dancer, and actor, MJ also has impeccable stunt skills—she received hand-to-hand combat training from none other than hero Captain America himself. She's also owned and managed nightclubs in New York City and Chicago, Illinois. She briefly wore the Iron Spider suit Tony Stark designed for Peter to help defeat the foe Regent. Most recently, MJ has been hired by Stark Industries as Tony's executive administrator, a job at which she has excelled.

Friends, allies, and role models:
Pepper Potts (p90), **Ironheart** (p114)

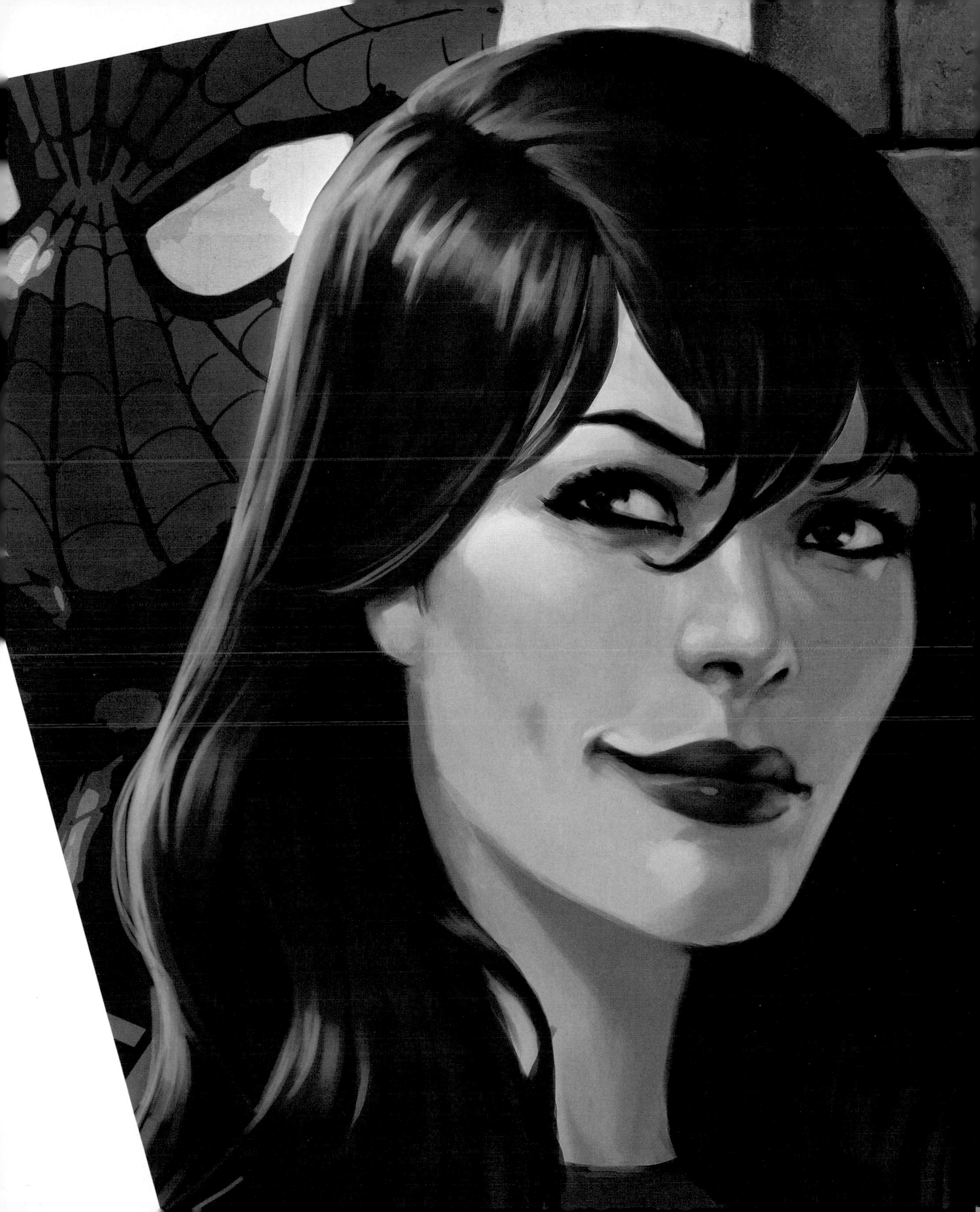

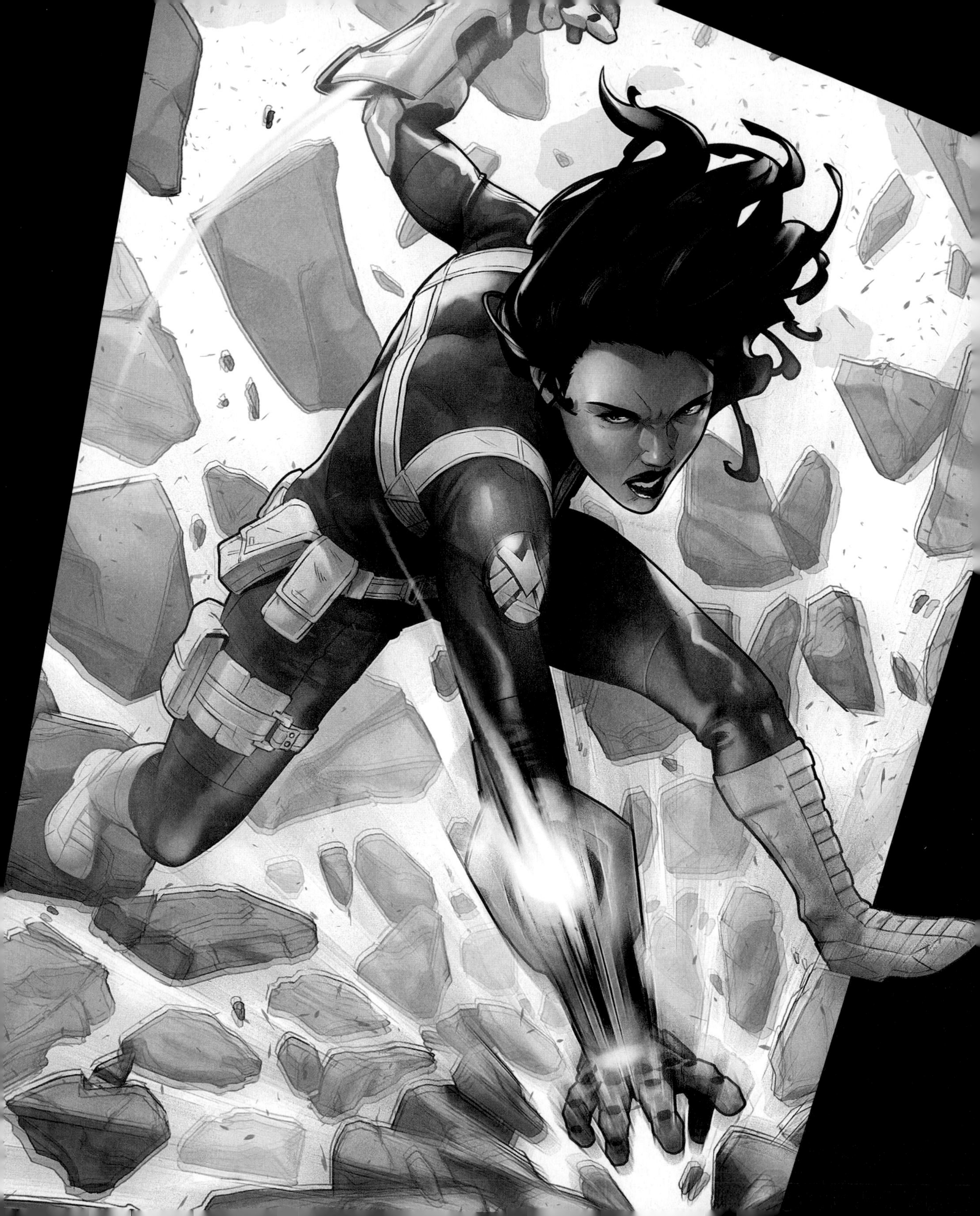

QUAKE

"So, who wants to come with me and **save the world?**"

Daisy Johnson was adopted at seven months old and raised with no knowledge of her biological parents. It wasn't until an incident as a teenager that she discovered she had special powers that allowed her to create earthquakes, and to withstand the force of those vibrations. Her powers brought her to the attention of Nick Fury—the director of government organization S.H.I.E.L.D. Fury revealed that Daisy had inherited the Inhuman powers of her mother and the altered DNA of her villainous medical researcher father, Calvin Zabo, aka Mr. Hyde.

Daisy became a loyal S.H.I.E.L.D. agent, gaining Level 10 security clearance by the age of 17 and later becoming director herself. Her training makes her an expert martial artist and markswoman, and a skilled surveillance officer, while her Inhuman genes give her enhanced strength, stamina, speed, and reaction times. She helped the Avengers defeat the powerful mutant Magneto by causing a vibration in his brain that made him lose consciousness. It was at this time that she suggested she be known by the code name Quake.

Friends, allies, and role models:
Maria Hill (p24), **Sharon Carter** (p42), **Mockingbird** (p72), **Moon Girl** (p110)

AURORA

"There is **always hope. For all** of us."

Canadian Jeanne-Marie Beaubier was tragically separated from her twin brother at a very young age. As a teenager, she found a new love for life when she discovered she could fly at supersonic speeds. But the teachers at Jeanne-Marie's strict girls' school punished her for her mutant abilities and she developed Dissociative Identity Disorder, displaying two distinct personalities: the shy, introverted Jeanne-Marie, and the extroverted, superhuman "Aurora."

X-Men Super Hero Wolverine took notice of Aurora in Montréal when he found her using her superhuman speed to fight off robbers late at night. Impressed by her skills, he recommended Aurora to the Canadian government, who were assembling their very first Super Hero team: Alpha Flight. Aurora was then reunited with her long-lost twin, Jean-Paul, who had joined the team as the super-powered "Northstar." With the help of Jean-Paul and her team, Aurora has gained greater control of her personalities, and she has kept Canada safe from evil many times. Aurora was recently a member of Captain Marvel's Alpha Flight space program, and has also joined NASA.

Friends, allies, and role models:
Captain Marvel (p12), **America Chavez** (p56), **Rogue** (p78)

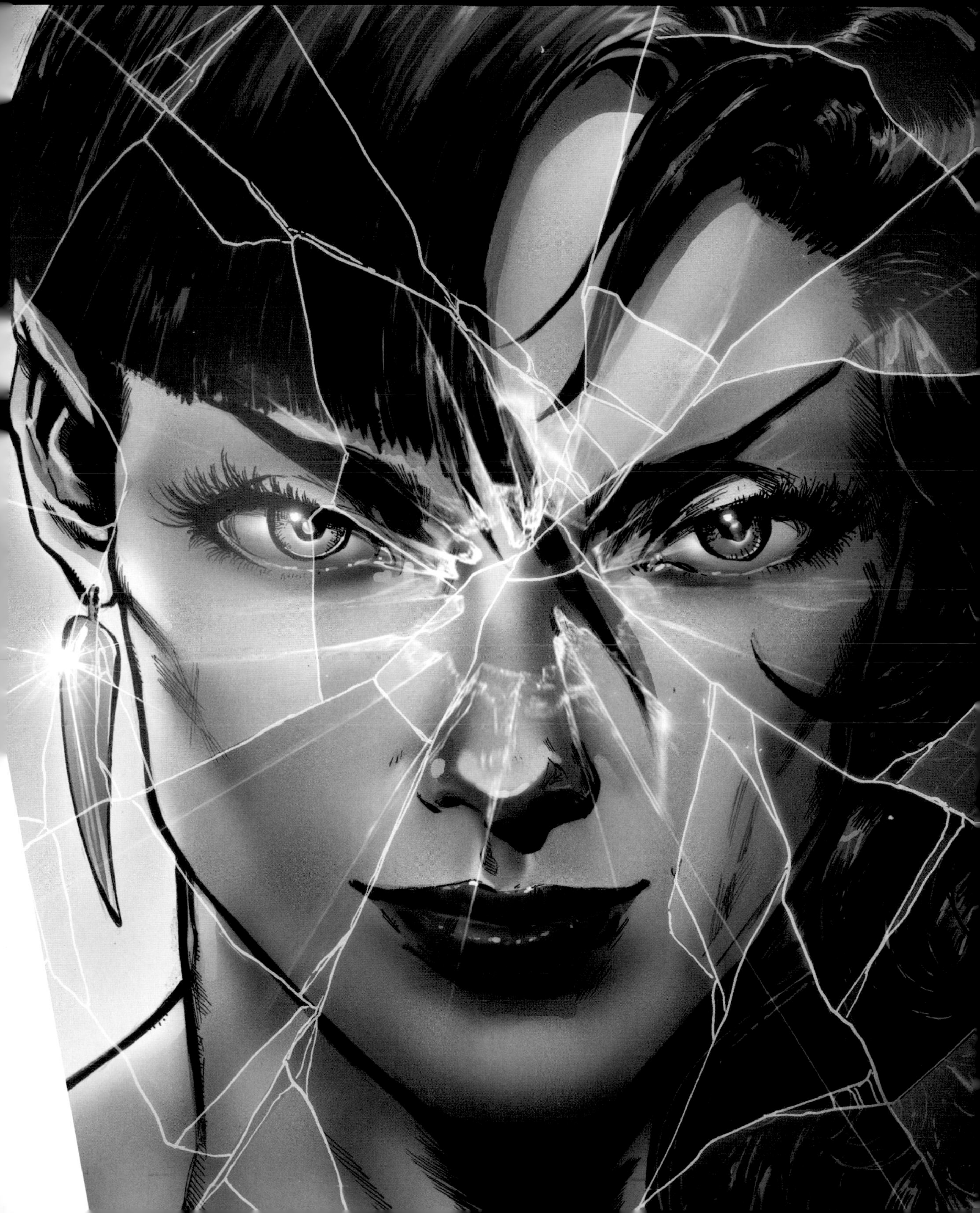

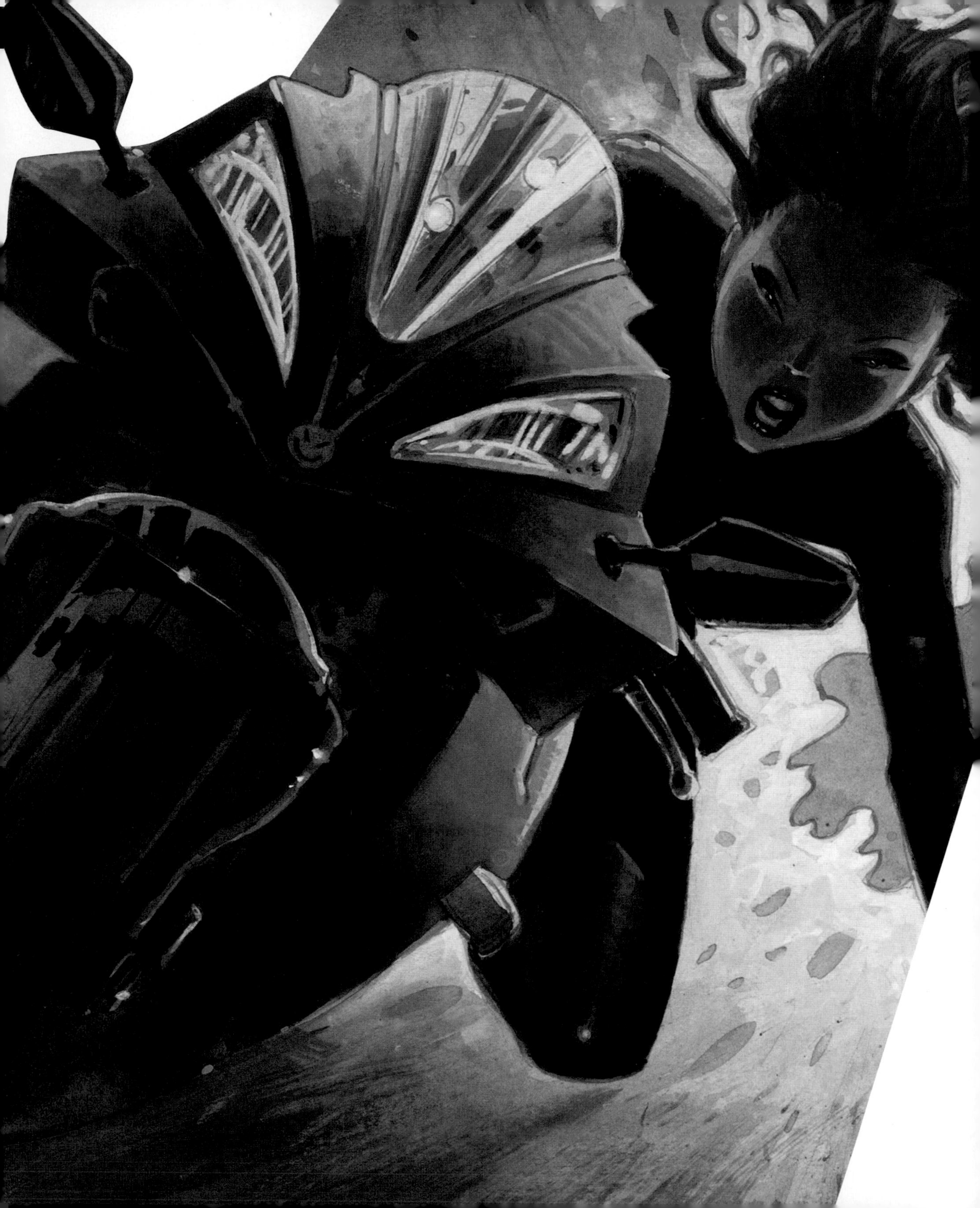

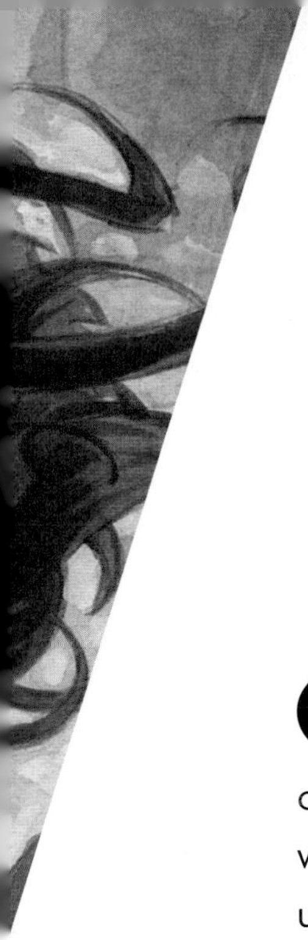

COLLEEN WING

"We never should have been heroes for hire... We should have just been heroes."

Colleen Wing was born to a professor father from New York City, and a Japanese mother descended from a long line of samurai warriors. When her mom passed away and her dad was too busy at Columbia University to raise her, Colleen grew up with her maternal grandfather, Kenji Ozawa, in Japan's northern mountains. Kenji, a former member of the Japanese secret service, trained Colleen in the ways of the samurai. As a result, Colleen is an expert with Kenji's thousand-year-old katana sword, and can focus her energy to enhance her strength and to speed up her body's healing.

On returning to New York as an adult, Colleen became fast friends with police officer Misty Knight. Together, they started their own private investigation business under the name Knightwing Restorations Ltd. They have also taken on the nickname "Daughters of the Dragon," first mockingly bestowed upon them by a foe. Colleen and Misty have helped each other through the toughest of times—while keeping the streets safe from villainy, of course—and have become even closer friends in the process.

Friends, allies, and role models:
Valkyrie (p28), **Jessica Jones** (p34), **Misty Knight** (p60)

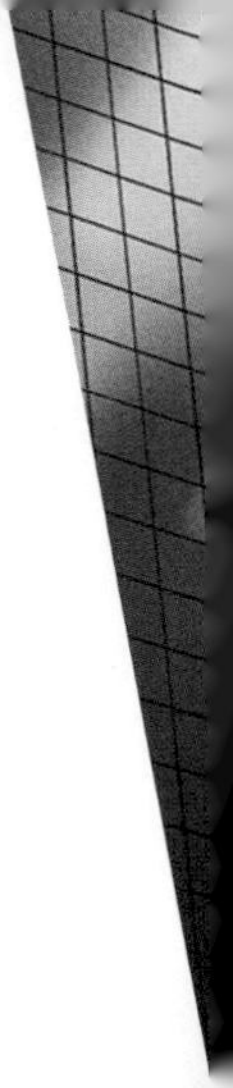

MADAME WEB

“We’re Force Works, out of Ventura, California. We came to help.”

When she agreed to take part in a secret government “athletic study,” single mother Julia Carpenter didn’t realize she was actually signing up for an injection of spider venom and plant extracts. She emerged with advanced spider-powers. As Spider-Woman (and later Arachne), Julia could stick to walls and make webbing, not through any physical means, but rather by manipulating matter with her mind. She fought alongside the West Coast Avengers and the Canada-based Omega Flight, and helped to found Force Works—a team that, combining the powers of Scarlet Witch and a supercomputer, attempted to thwart crimes before they ever occurred.

Julia took on a third identity when the powerful psychic Cassandra Webb died and passed along her skills and her name, Madame Web. In this new role, Julia is blind but has strong mind-reading and prophetic abilities. Having handed her old Spider-Woman costume down to Anya Corazon, Julia now wears a long, red trench coat and shades. She is able to read the Web of Life and Destiny, which connects all those with spider-powers, for signs of coming danger.

Friends, allies, and role models:
Mockingbird (p72), **Scarlet Witch** (p104), **Spider-Girl** (p120)

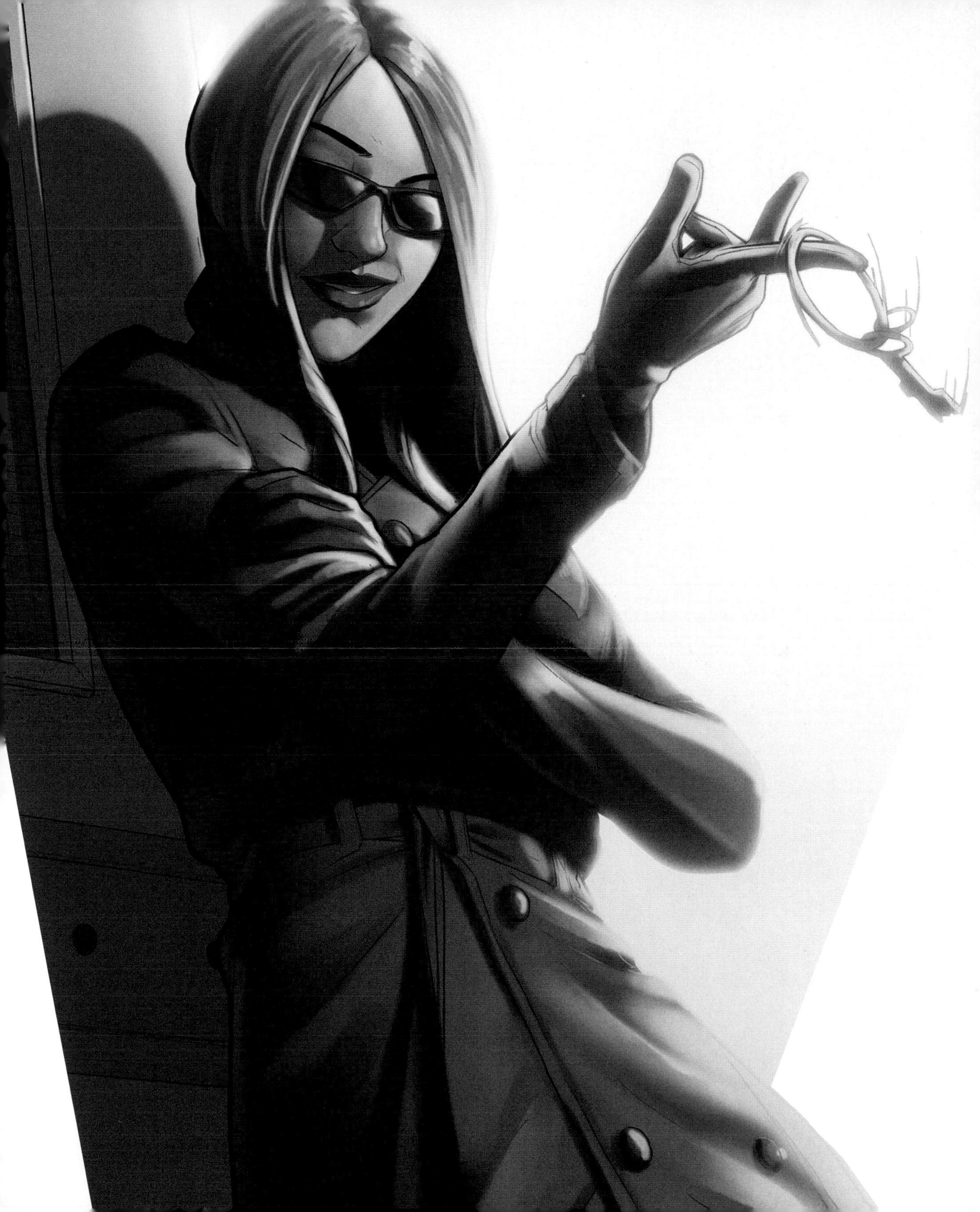

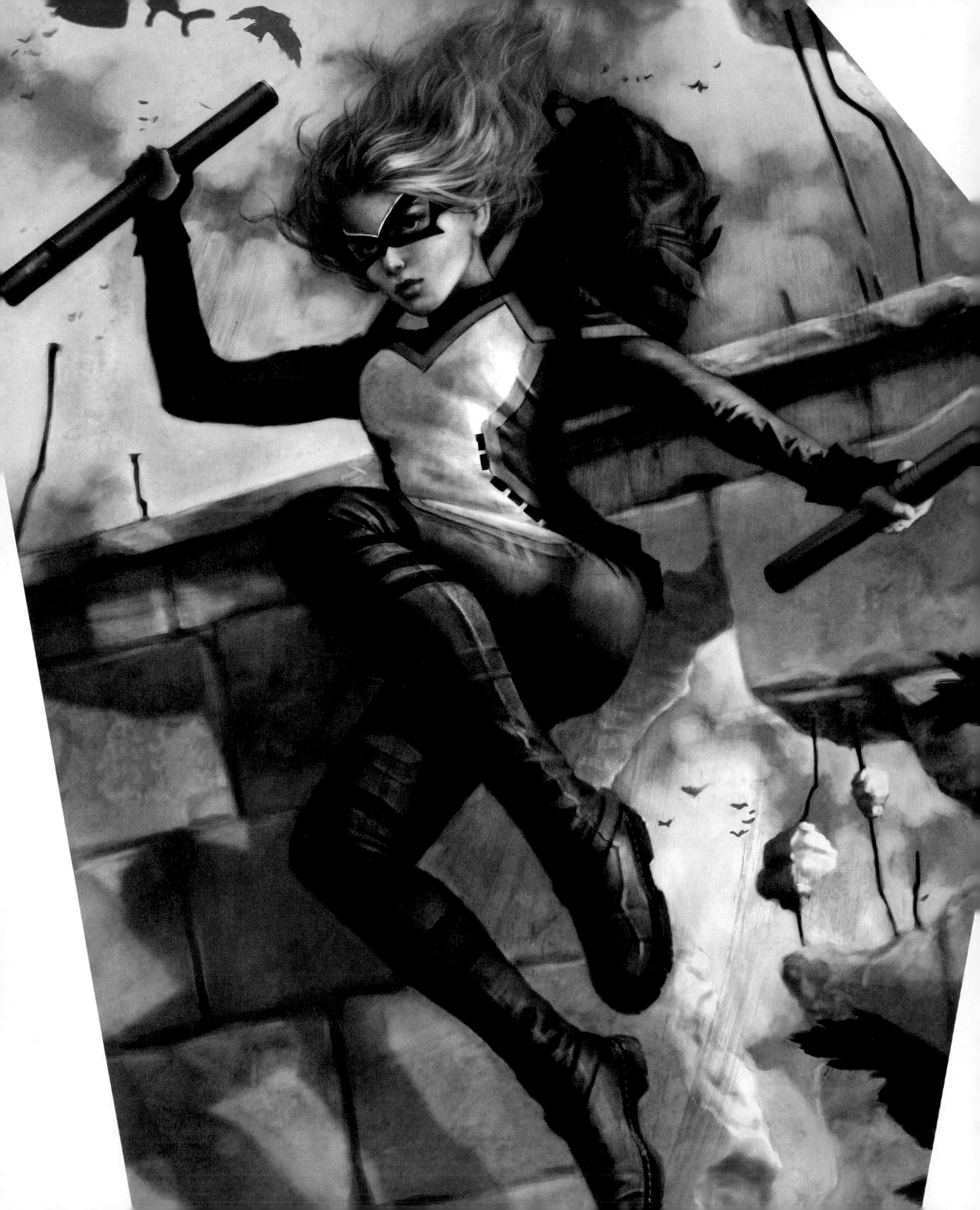

MOCKINGBIRD

"Excuse me, we were in the middle of a heroic gesture on behalf of mankind."

Shortly after graduating with a PhD in biology, Dr. Barbara "Bobbi" Morse joined the U.S. government's "Project Gladiator" to recreate the Super-Soldier Serum that gave Captain America his powers. Bobbi's work gained S.H.I.E.L.D.'s attention and she was recruited as Agent 19. Trained in martial arts, hand-to-hand combat, and espionage, Agent 19 became nearly as dangerous in battle as Captain America himself. Bobbi is witty and sarcastic, using humor to cope with difficult situations and often mocking opponents in the heat of battle—thus earning her code name "Mockingbird."

Mockingbird has protected S.H.I.E.L.D.'s integrity, rooting out corruption and double agents. She has also fought alongside the West Coast, Great Lakes, and New Avengers teams. In a life-saving procedure, Bobbi was injected with a combination of the Super-Soldier Serum and former S.H.I.E.L.D. director Nick Fury's life-extending Infinity Formula, which improved her strength, speed, and healing abilities. She uses a pair of battle staves when fighting, either separately or connected to form one staff. Anyone calling her Barbara does so at their own peril!

Friends, allies, and role models:
Black Widow (p18), **Maria Hill** (p24), **Spider-Woman—Jessica Drew** (p102)

AYO

"You do not want to trifle with me."

Proud, hot-tempered Ayo is a warrior with nerves of steel and a fierce devotion to the people and politics she cares about. Born in the African kingdom of Wakanda, Ayo was raised by her father to fight without mercy, just like her brothers. She joined the *Dora Milaje*, a squad of female bodyguards who protect the Black Panther, Wakanda's monarch and defender. Ayo received tough training in combat and warfare tactics. The path was not always smooth, since she disliked taking orders and frequently argued with the squad's captain, Aneka—though the two soon fell deeply in love.

Ayo was horrified when Aneka was arrested for killing a wicked chieftain, and tried to plead Aneka's case to the Queen Mother, Ramonda. When this failed, Ayo bravely risked her own life to rescue Aneka from prison. Both women escaped in stolen armor, turning their backs on the *Dora Milaje* and the Black Panther, King T'Challa, who they believed was no longer a worthy monarch. They became known as the Midnight Angels, and eventually led a revolt to fight for freedom and their fellow countrywomen. Ayo always follows her heart, driven by her love for Aneka and her country. Impulsive and impatient, Ayo is unafraid to question those in power.

Friends, allies, and role models:
Queen Ramonda (p36), **Shuri** (p100)

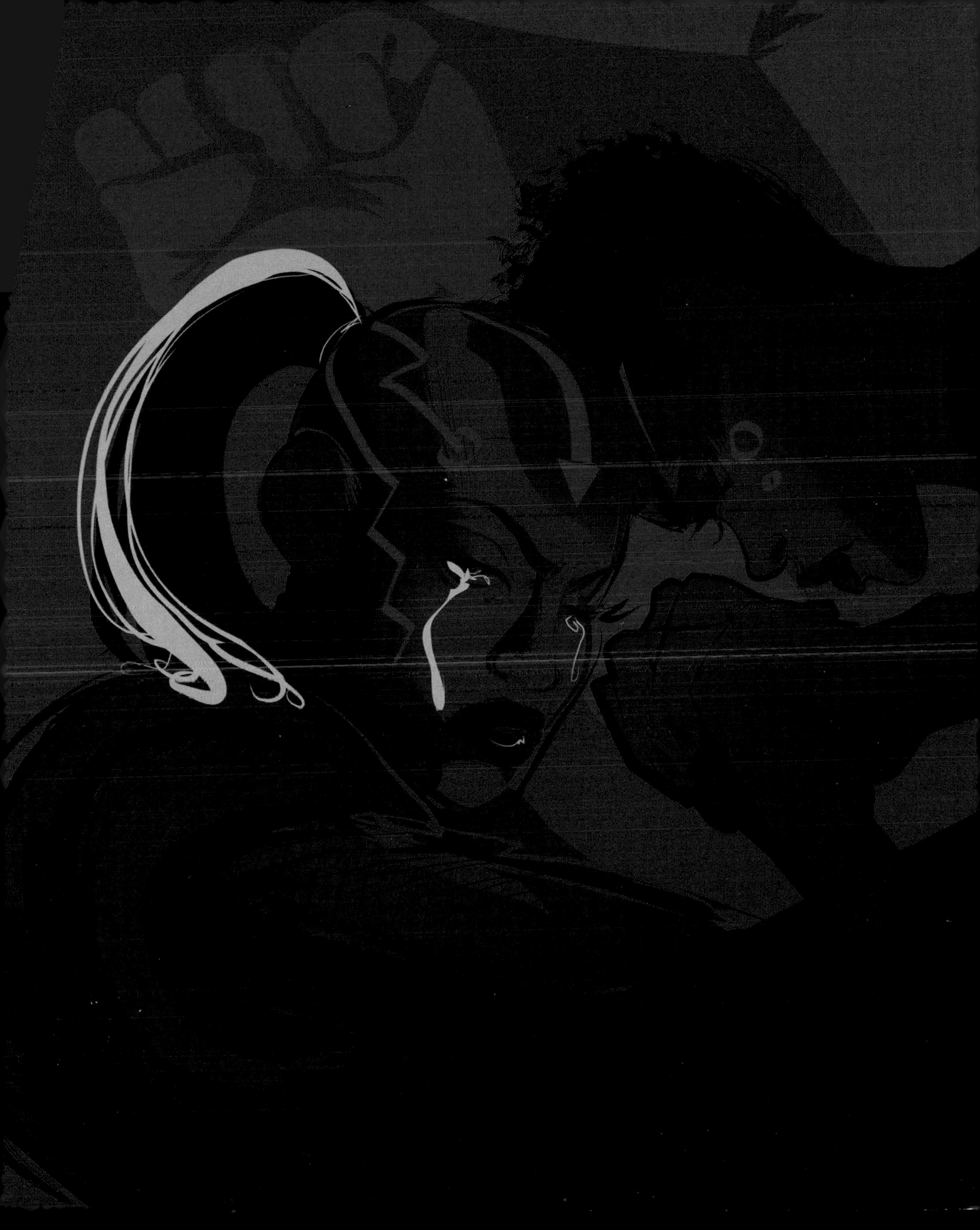

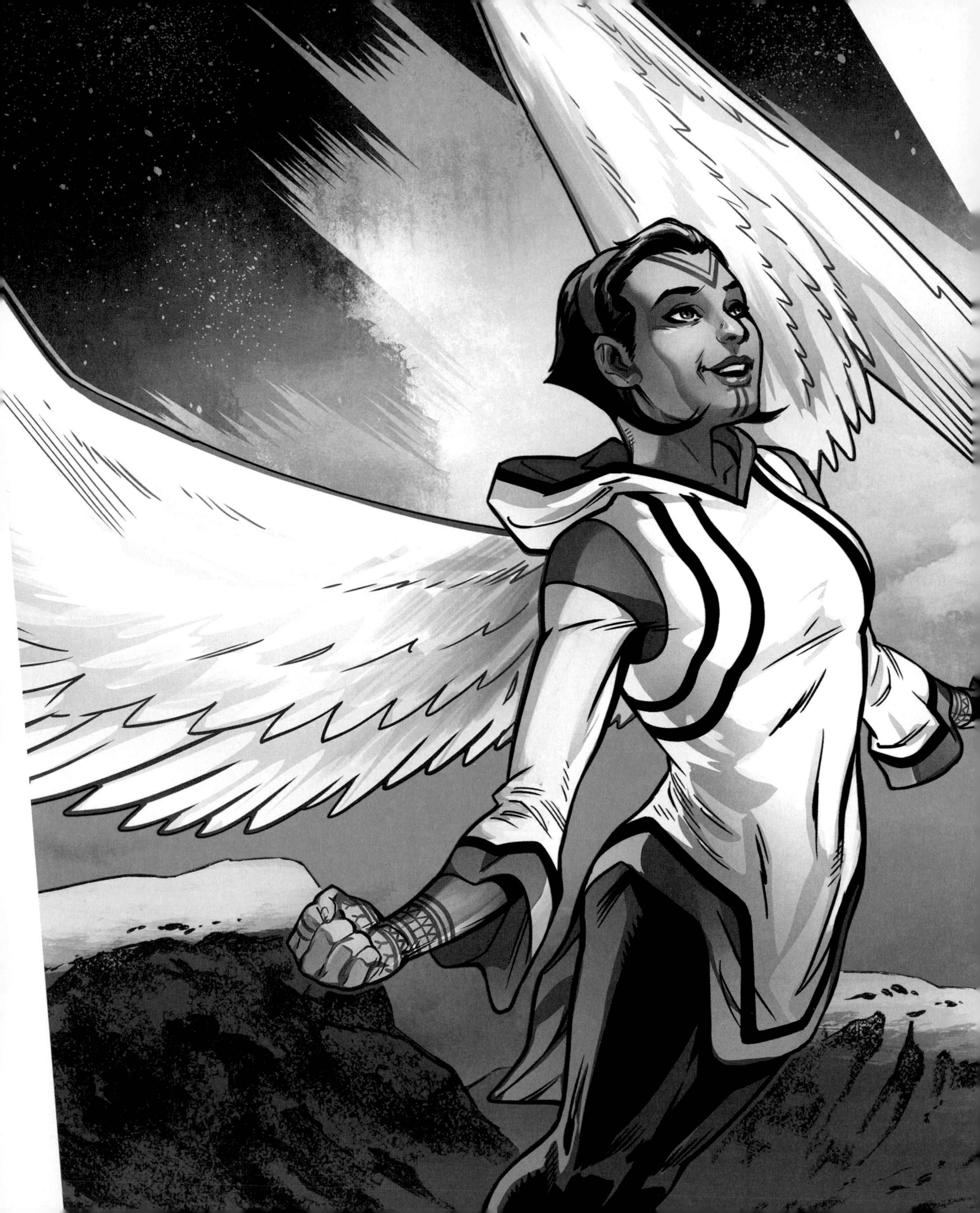

SNOWGUARD

"Now here I am... filled with **spirits** and **songs** I've never heard before."

Brave, independent Amka Aliyak is a teenager with a fierce desire to help her community. Amka belongs to the Inuit people of Pangnirtung, a town in Canada's northernmost territory. When a mysterious factory was suddenly built against the local people's wishes, daring Amka climbed its fence to find out what was inside, unafraid of the patrolling security droids. She discovered that the Sila—the spirit force of the land, sky, and weather—was being held captive by a villain who sought to exploit its energies. Amka freed the Sila from its prison, despite the danger to herself. In the process, she was filled with the spirit's magical energies. These grant her shape-shifting powers and the ability to grow animal features at will, such as claws, antlers, and even huge wings that allow her to fly.

The Champions, a team of young Super Heroes who seek to right the wrongs of Earth's previous generations, ask Amka to join them. At first, Amka is worried about leaving her mom at home without care. However, her mom encourages her to seize this opportunity to join the team and spread the stories of the Inuit people and their lands.

Friends, allies, and role models:
Ms. Marvel (p26), **Wasp—Nadia Van Dyne** (p108)

ROGUE

"Truth be told, I **used** to be quite a stinker, but **I cleaned up mah act** since then."

Anna Marie LeBeau was nicknamed Rogue as a teenager in Mississippi because of her misbehavior. The first time she kissed someone, Rogue discovered that she was a mutant and could temporarily absorb the life energy of anyone with whom she came into direct contact. Rogue's power could be lethal; the longer she touched someone, the more of their powers, memories, and abilities she gained. Growing bitter that her power was more of a curse than a blessing, Rogue donned gloves and joined the Brotherhood of Evil Mutants, where she was taken in by Mystique and Destiny.

Rogue eventually realized she had been fighting for the wrong side and was welcomed into the X-Men, where she gained her teammates' trust. She is now one of the most valued and experienced X-Men, commanding teams such as the Avengers Unity Division, a collaboration between the Avengers and the X-Men. Through years of training she has gained better control over her abilities, and often travels with her longtime love and new husband, Gambit. When she speaks she has a charming and confident southern American drawl.

Friends, allies, and role models:
Jubilee (p40), **Aurora** (p66), **Kitty Pryde** (p116), **Dazzler** (p124)

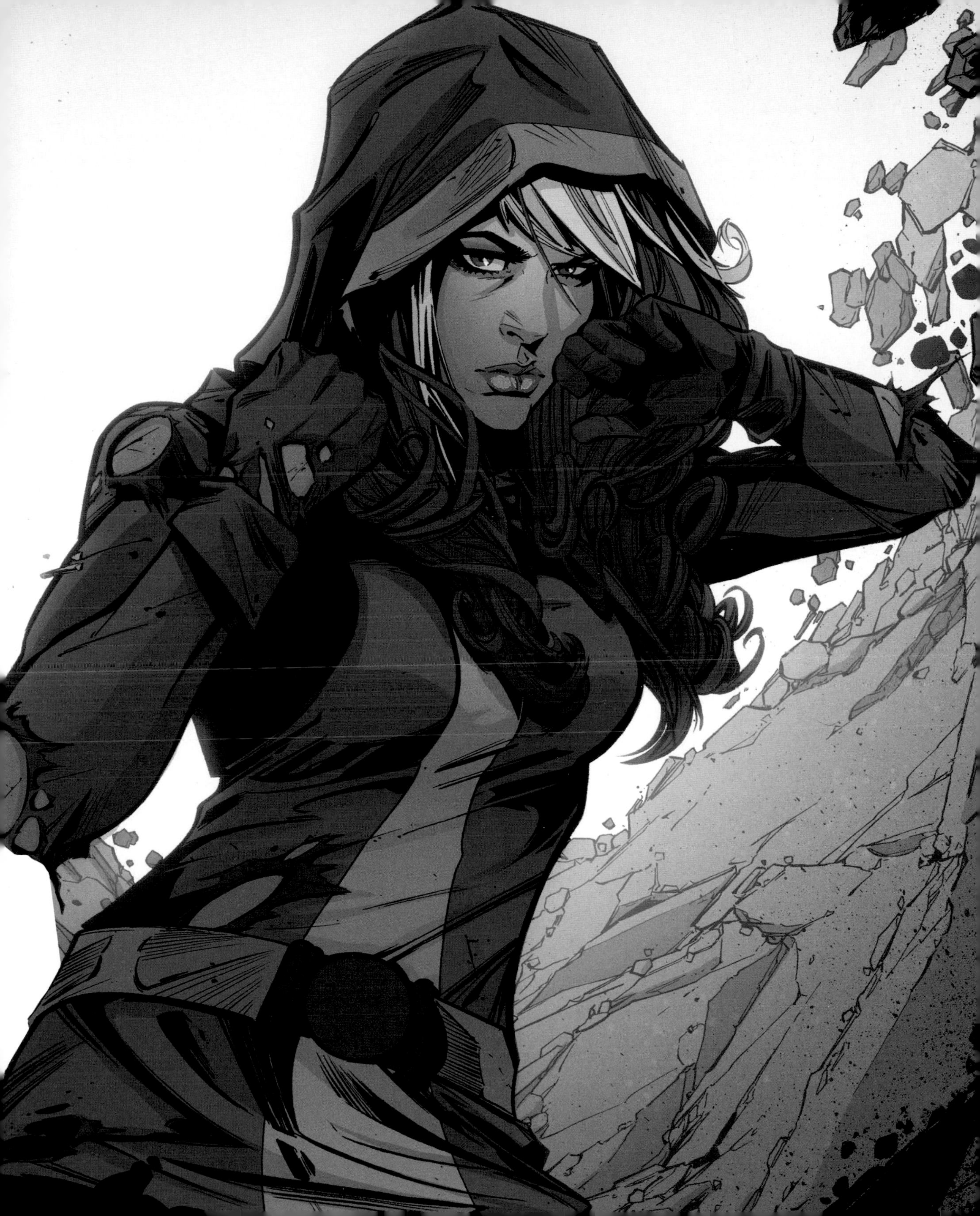

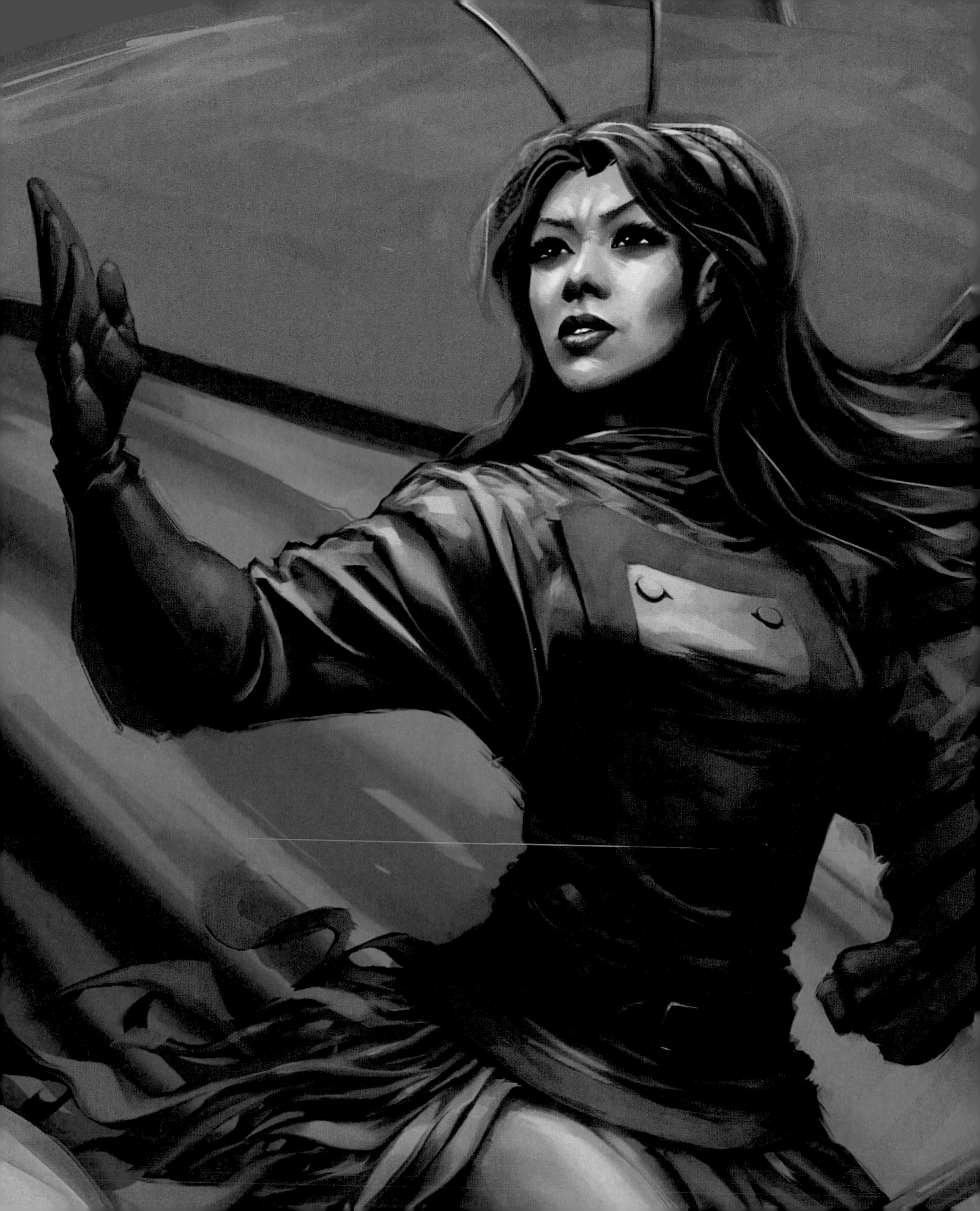

COMPASSIONATE

In worlds of war and strife, expressing kindness is often the most radical move of all. Everybody can learn from the empathy in Mantis; the motherly compassion in Medusa; the willingness to understand everyone—even your foes— in Squirrel Girl. These heroes demonstrate that mercy and sympathy are two of the strongest super-powers.

◄ Mantis (p84)

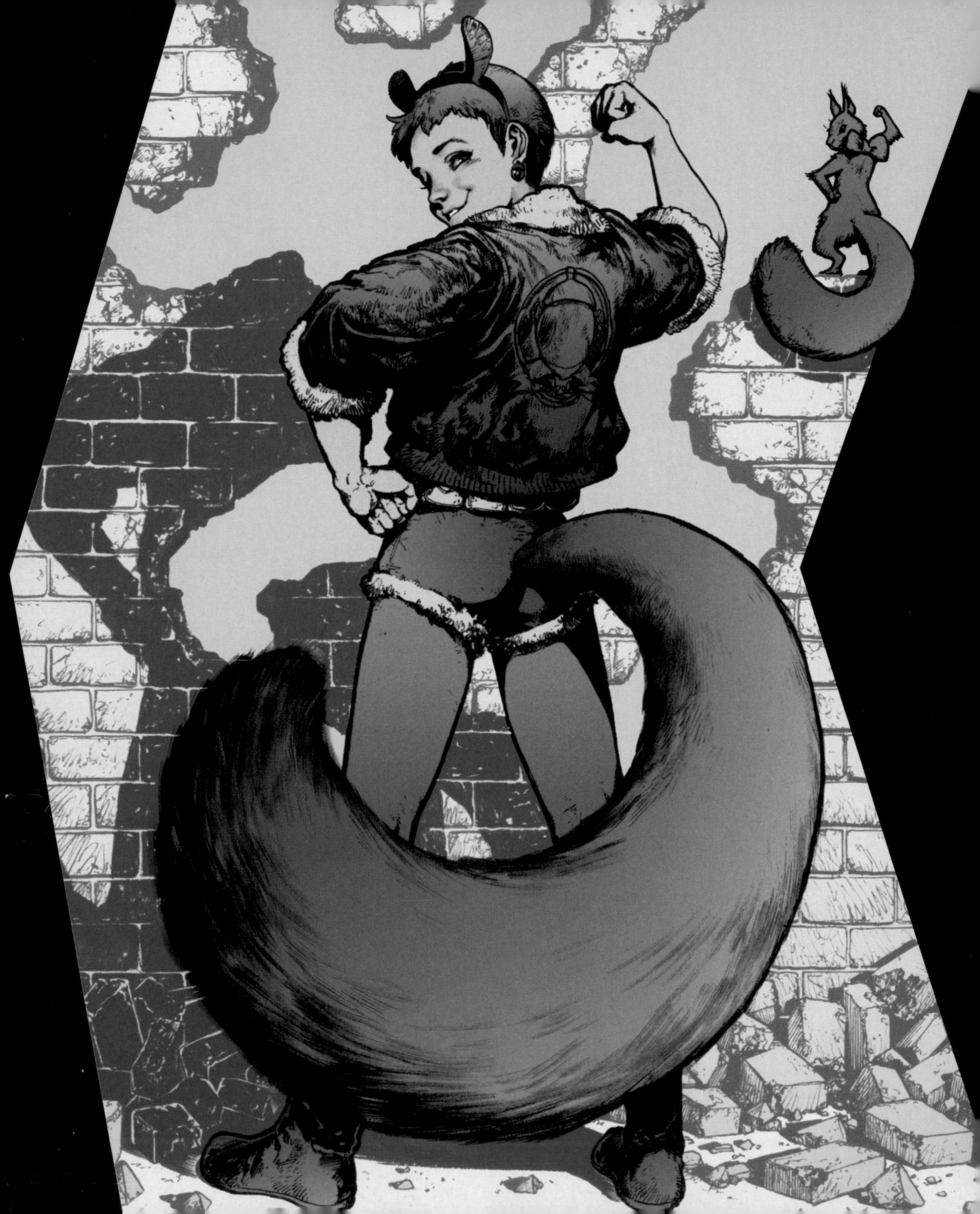

SQUIRREL GIRL

"We all have anxieties, but—and this may sound crazy—they're actually kinda what makes us awesome!"

Fast-talking, high-kicking teen Doreen Green first drew Super Hero attention when she tried to talk her way into the Avengers. Having overcome bullies in high school, she proceeded to triumph over Iron Man's nemesis Doctor Doom, but that wasn't enough to secure the Avengers' approval. Moving to New York City to fight crime and keep Central Park safe, she soon attracted another team-up—the Great Lakes Avengers—when she rescued them from a mugging.

Genetic scientists are unsure exactly what gifted Doreen a tail that can grab onto objects and teeth that can chew through wood. Her other extraordinary abilities include super-speed and strength, and an affinity with wildlife, such as the ability to talk to squirrels—including Tippy-Toe, her BSFF (Best Squirrel Friend Forever). Plucky Doreen loves putting Super Villains in their place. She is just as likely to be found winning poker games as babysitting for Super Heroes, going to computer programming classes, or hanging out with her loyal friends Nancy Whitehead, Chipmunk Hunk, and Koi Boi.

Friends, allies, and role models:
Ms. Marvel (p26), **Jessica Jones** (p34), **Dr. Toni Ho** (p118)

MANTIS

"This one is the Celestial Madonna.
I go where I wish."

With powers of telepathy, empathy, and chlorokinesis (the ability to control plants), Mantis acts as a field agent and counselor for the Guardians of the Galaxy team. A kind oddball, Mantis often refers to herself as "this one" instead of "I" because of her unusual upbringing. To keep her safe from her crime lord uncle, her German father hid the infant Mantis at a temple in Vietnam, her mother's homeland. There, Mantis was raised by the peace-loving Priests of Pama—Kree aliens exiled to Earth for protecting a telepathic plant race named the Cotati. The Priests trained Mantis to become their "Celestial Madonna," destined to give birth to a child who would bring universal peace.

Mantis's connection to the Cotati gifts her with astonishing mental powers, and on mastering martial arts, she becomes so skillful that she defeats many larger male opponents. She is given the name "Mantis," after the praying mantis insect whose females kill the males of their species. She is so effective in battle that Mantis has even knocked down the thunder god Thor with a single blow.

Friends, allies, and role models:
Gamora (p48), **Scarlet Witch** (p104), **She-Hulk** (p106)

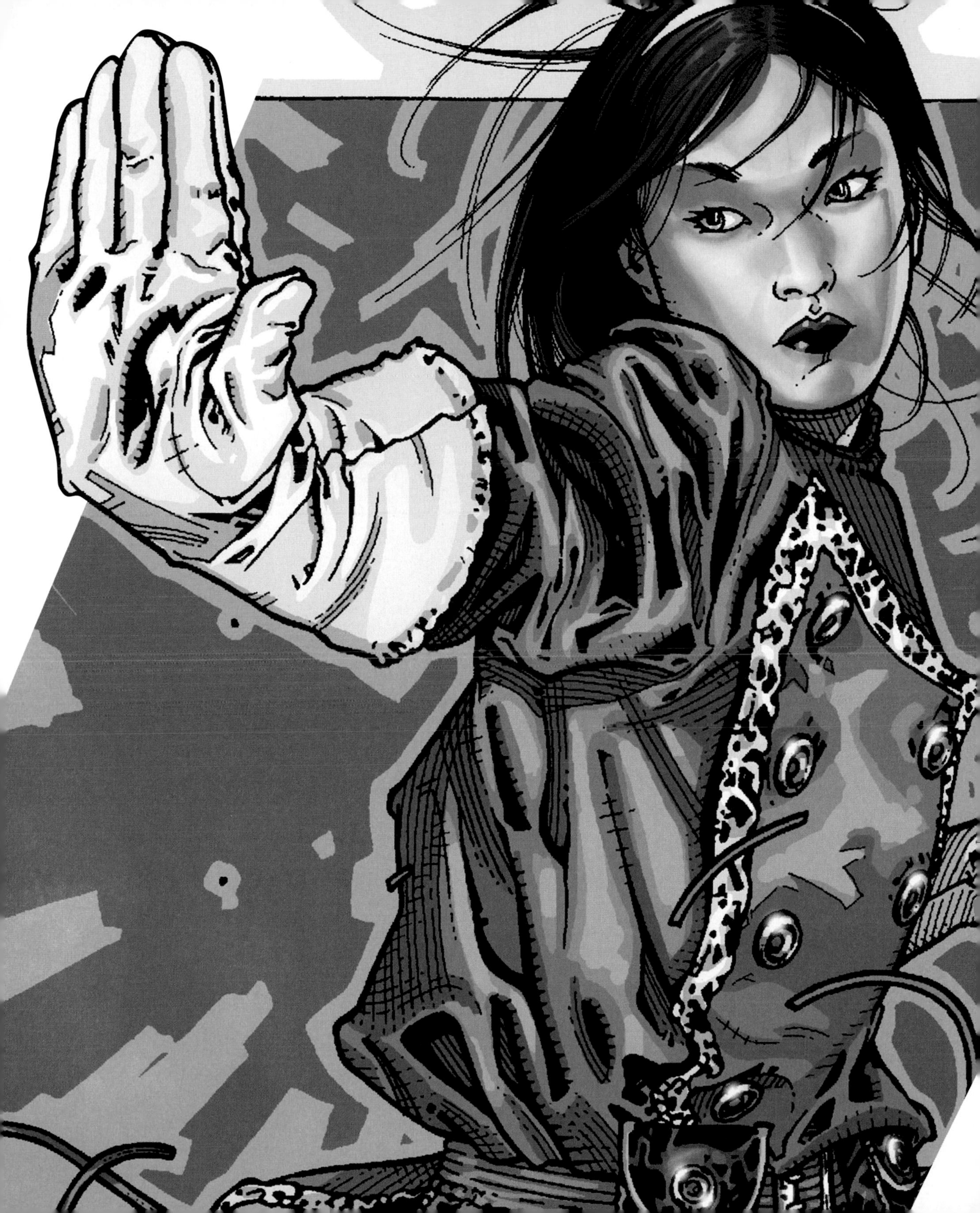

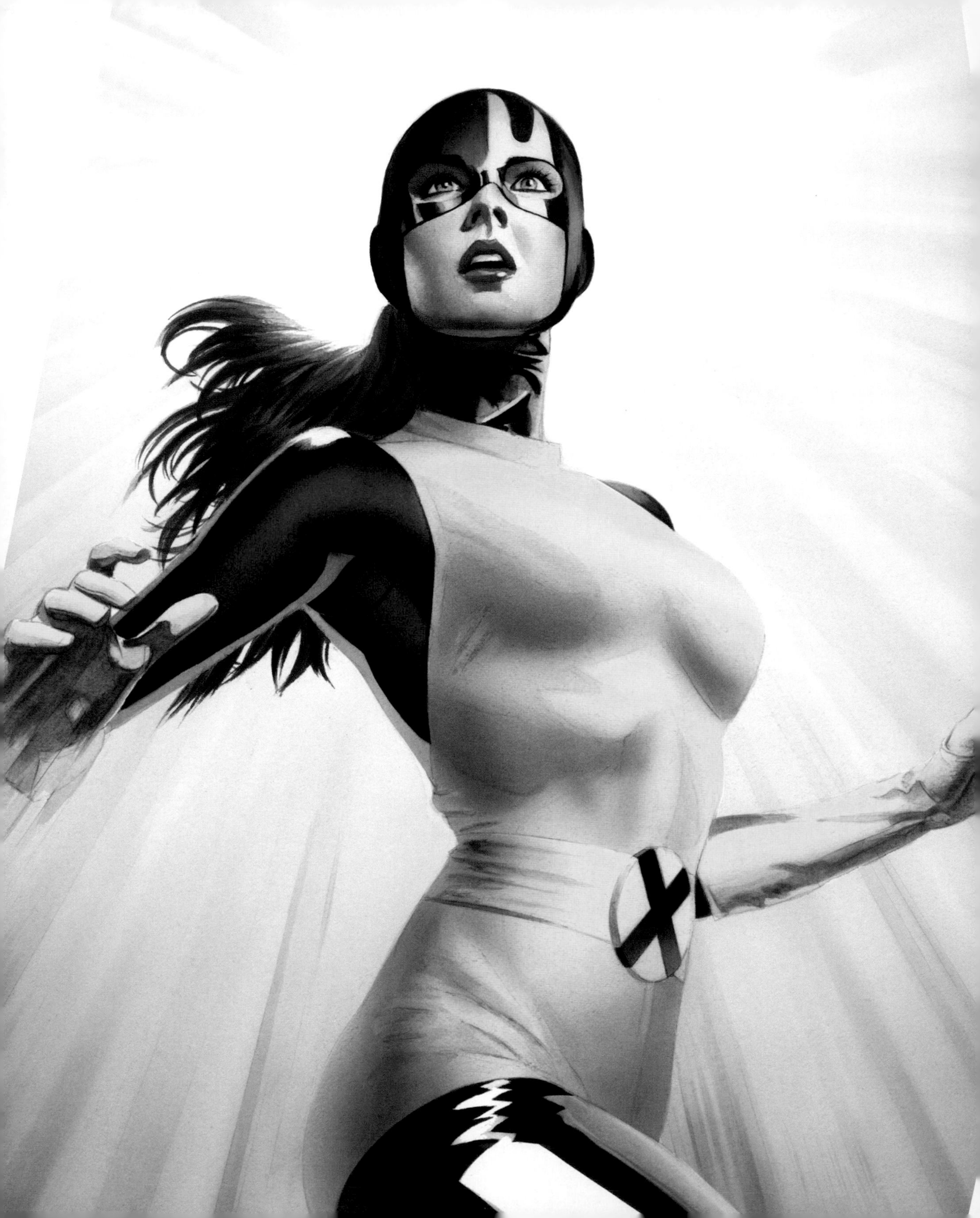

JEAN GREY

"I refuse to accept this world for how it is. I'm going to change it."

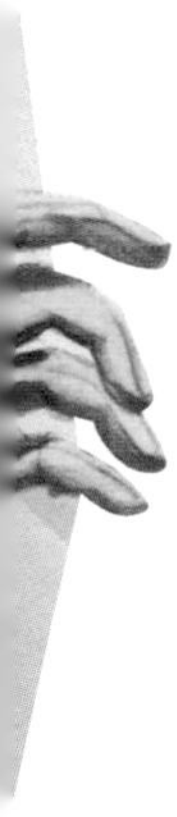

Jean Grey is a mutant with telepathic and telekinetic abilities, able to manipulate objects with her mind. After attending Charles Xavier's School for Gifted Youngsters, she became the first woman to join the X-Men, briefly going by the code name "Marvel Girl." While on a mission in space, Jean saved her teammates by making a bargain with a mysterious entity made of cosmic energy, named the Phoenix Force. From that moment, the Phoenix shared Jean's body and consciousness, granting her cosmic powers: she could create fire, survive in space, and travel through wormholes. Jean has even died and been revived many times by the Phoenix Force. The Phoenix was often corrupted into the evil Dark Phoenix, carrying out terrible acts beyond Jean's control. However, she is now back from the dead and free of the Phoenix Force.

Jean has a long-standing, occasionally challenging relationship with fellow X-Man, Cyclops. At one point they were married, and they have two children in alternate realities of the future. Kind Jean has a strong, sisterlike bond with her X-Men teammate, Storm.

Friends, allies, and role models:
Storm (p16), **Kitty Pryde** (p116), **Dazzler** (p124)

FIREBIRD

"Be unique because you are unique!"

Bonita Juarez was an ordinary social worker walking in the Albuquerque desert in New Mexico when a radioactive meteor landed nearby. It gave her extraordinary fire powers, or pyrokinesis. Miraculously unhurt, she discovered she could now summon and direct intense flames and rushing winds. She also gained fighting skills, self-healing powers, and the ability to fly. As a devout Catholic, Bonita was soon using her powers for good and to stop criminals—one of whom described her as "Firebird," a creature from Native American legend. From this moment on, Bonita decided to take this name for herself and become a Super Hero.

Initially joining the Avengers by accident—when she intercepted and responded to a call meant for them—Firebird has since fought alongside them many times, and with Southern State Super Hero group the Rangers. Bonita has worked hard to balance her religious beliefs with her superpowers, and has used her empathetic instincts to counsel other heroes, such as Thor, god of thunder, and downhearted biochemist Hank Pym. She can sometimes be found fighting as "La Espirita" (the Spirit) or as the Avenger of Texas.

Friends, allies, and role models:
Jessica Jones (p34), **Spectrum** (p52), **Mockingbird** (p72)

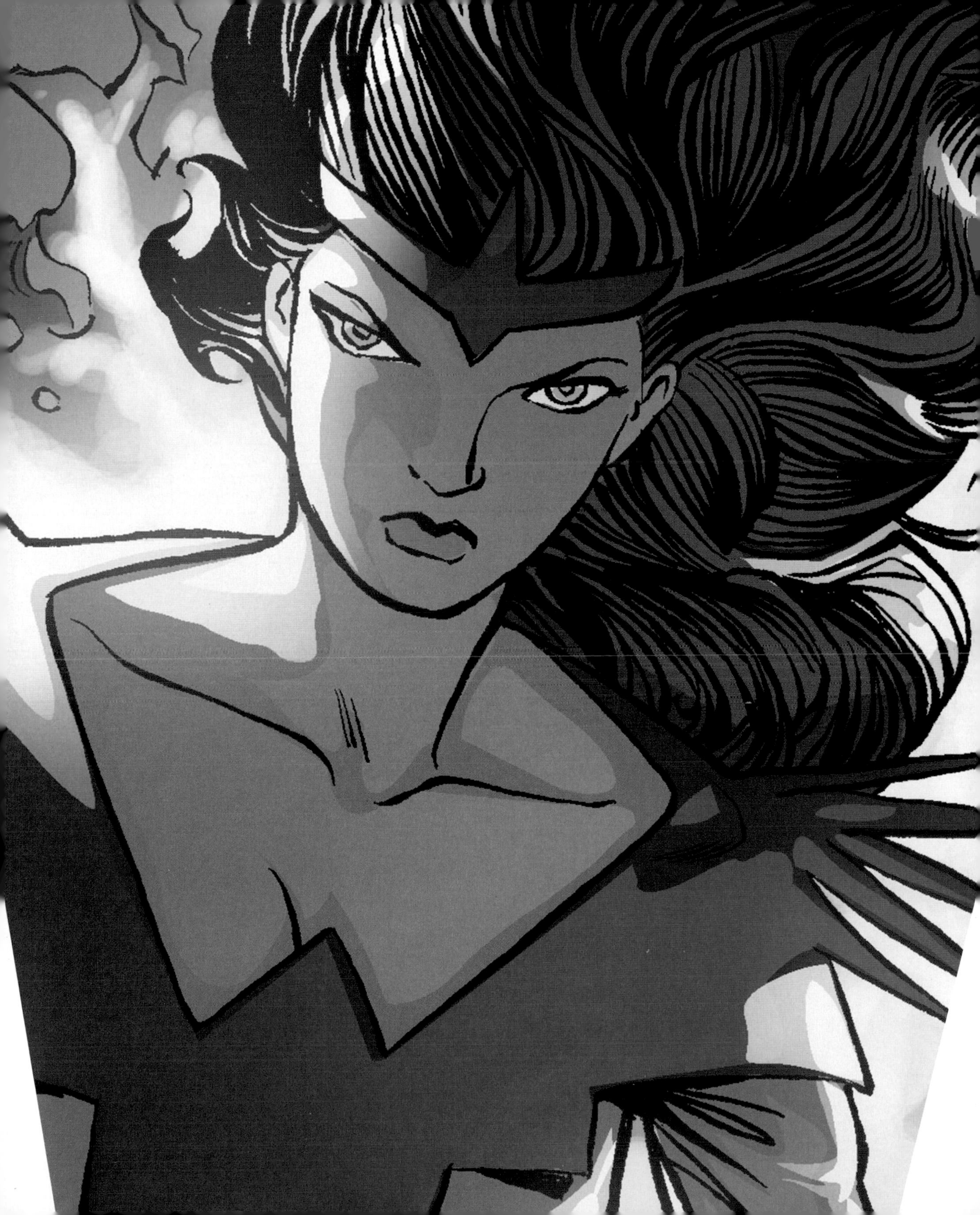

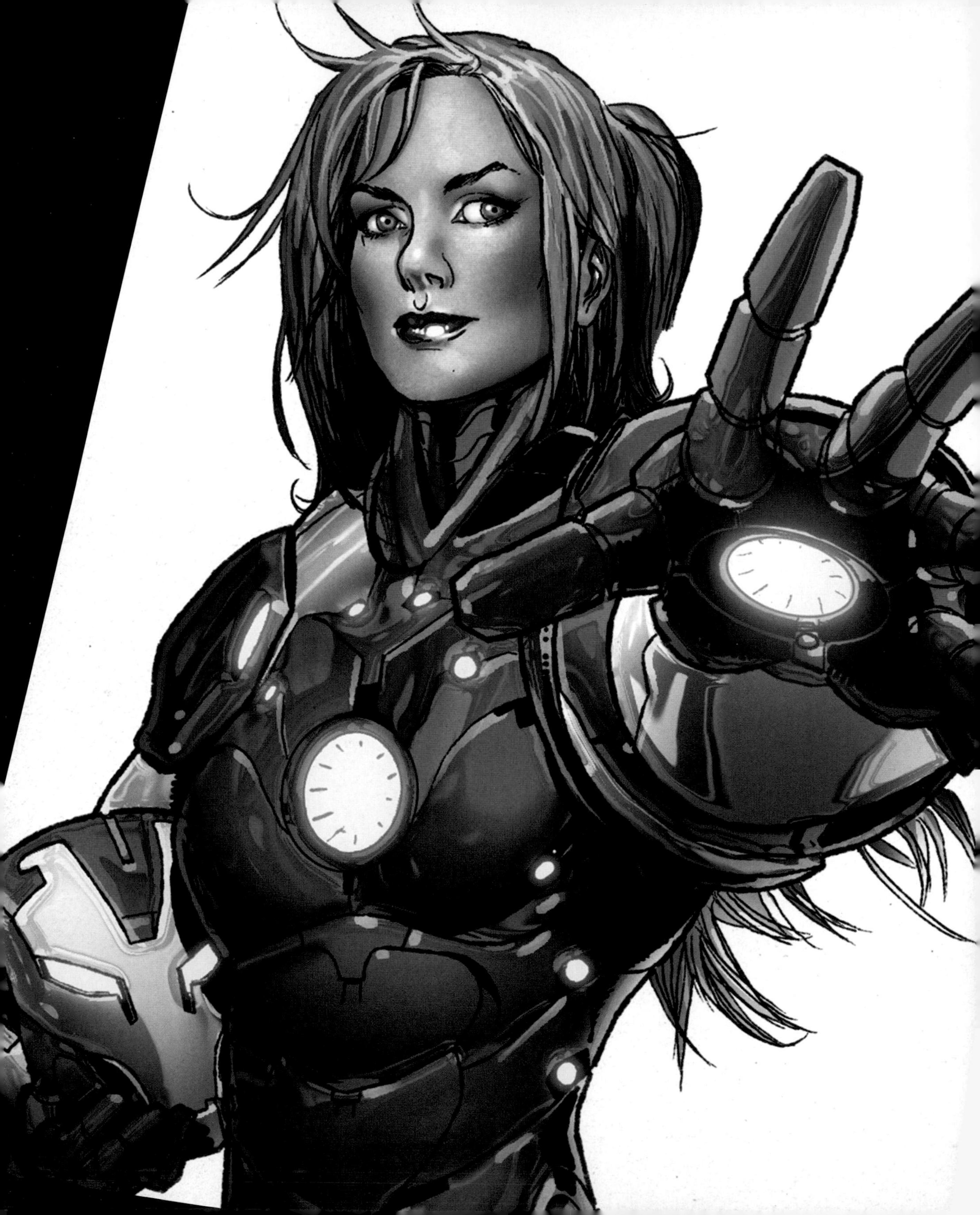

PEPPER POTTS

"How do I feel...?
Invincible."

Virginia Potts' freckles earned her the nickname "Pepper," but her skill inside the Iron Man suit won her the alter ego "Rescue." As the executive assistant of Tony Stark—aka Iron Man—Pepper became an invaluable member of Stark Industries, eventually taking charge of the business entirely. While working in Taipei, Pepper was injured in an explosion. In order to stop shrapnel from the blast traveling deeper inside her body, Pepper had a magnetic Repulsor Tech (R.T.) node fitted into her chest—similar to the reactor Tony wears.

The R.T. node, plus some other cybernetic enhancements, improves Pepper's strength, speed, and senses, and allows her to manipulate energy. She can also levitate and create force fields. Now, with a weapons-free Mark 1616 Iron Man suit built personally for her, Pepper has embraced Super Hero life as Rescue, focusing specifically on rescuing the civilian victims of Super Villain attacks. In addition to flying alongside power-suited heroes Iron Man and War Machine, Pepper is a mentor and close ally to Riri Williams, the teenage girl from Chicago better known as Ironheart.

Friends, allies, and role models:
Black Widow (p18), **Maria Hill** (p24), **Ironheart** (p114)

MEDUSA

"I am the face of the Inhuman nation... Being Inhuman can be... wonderful."

Queen Medusalith Amaquelin Boltagon (Medusa) rules the Inhuman race alongside her husband, Black Bolt. His frequent absences mean Medusa is often called upon to rule alone. She is fiercely protective and prepared to fight anybody who dares to oppose her, on behalf of her people and her son, Ahura.

Born into the Inhuman royal family in their hidden capital city Attilan on Earth, Medusa was raised to be a leader. The Inhumans are an advanced species of humans who gain their powers from the mutagenic Terrigen Mists. These mists made Medusa's hair tougher than steel and gave it the power to move at Medusa's will. As an Inhuman, Medusa is naturally super-fast and strong. She soon learned to use her hair in combat—as a whip, as ropes to bind up foes, and even to pick locks! The Inhumans have come into conflict with Earth's resident humans many times. When Attilan is destroyed, it is Medusa who seeks a new home for her people. And when her husband goes missing, she promises to never stop until she brings him home safe.

Friends, allies, and role models:
Captain Marvel (p12), **Wasp—Janet Van Dyne** (p46), **Singularity** (p94)

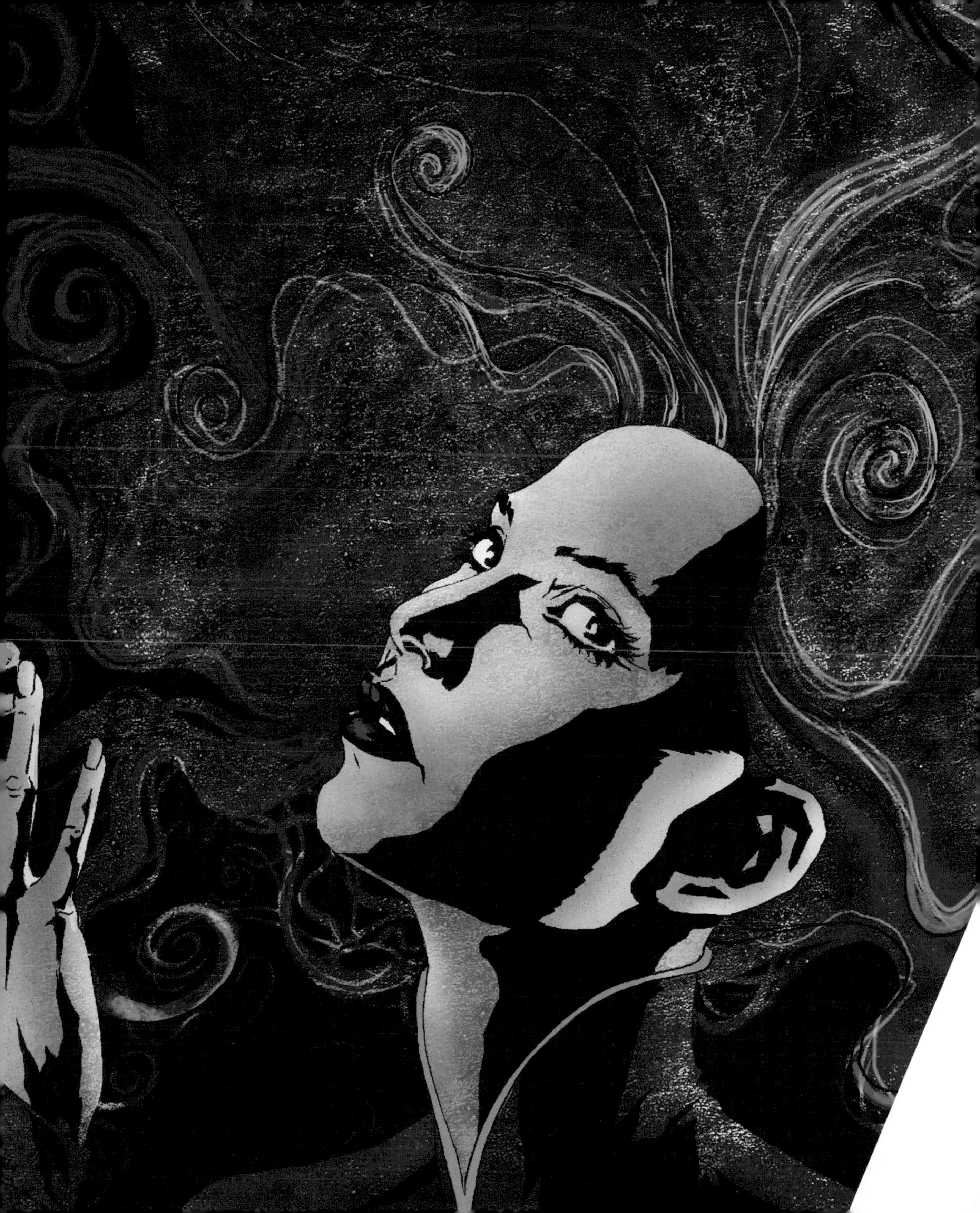

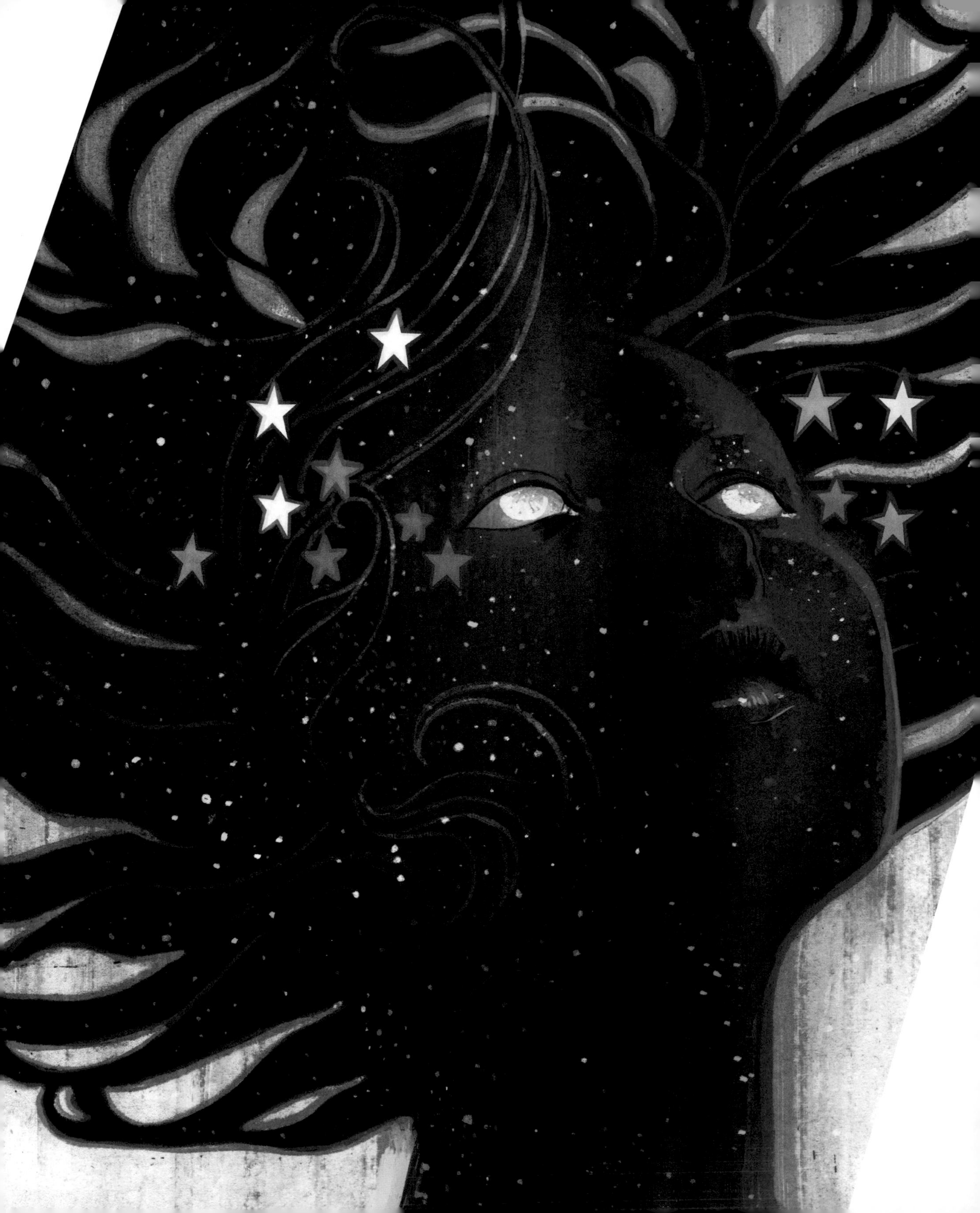

SINGULARITY

"We are a team. We are friends. We are heroes. And it is time we save the day."

When Earth's Mightiest Heroines unite and form A-Force in another world known as Arcadia, they are taken by surprise when a starry dimension in female form crashes into their midst. The visitor develops an emotional telepathic bond with Nico, the member of A-Force who first found her, and informs them that her name is Singularity.

From A-Force, Singularity learns about friendship, love, strength, bravery, and even heartbreak. Her powers are vast and other-worldly: she can absorb liquid and solid matter, cloak others in invisibility (thus hiding her teammates from danger), and can open portals to other realms. Unfortunately this can lead to tears in reality, and she quickly finds herself having to fight antimatter invaders. Singularity is bighearted, and quickly becomes attached to people. Her curious mind draws her to collecting objects like a magpie does. In a confusing world often filled with violence, Singularity promotes friendship, smiling, generosity, forgiveness, and hugs. She feels emotions deeply and appears to have chosen her current form for reasons that she cannot yet fathom.

Friends, allies, and role models:
Captain Marvel (p12), **Nico Minoru** (p30), **Medusa** (p92), **Dazzler** (p124)

KAROLINA DEAN

"I can finally stop pretending to be something I'm not."

Kind and gentle teenager Karolina Dean thought her parents being selfish Hollywood actors was unusual enough—but learning they were murderous, alien Super Villains in a group known as the Pride turned her life upside down. As did learning she too had inherited Majesdanian alien super-powers: flight, solar energy manipulation, and the ability to cast energy blasts in all the colors of the rainbow. Until this point, Karolina's true nature had been restrained by a specialized medical alert bracelet that she always wore. Turning her back on her parents' evil legacy, she ran away, took on the alias "Lucy in the Sky," and formed the Runaways with five other like-minded children of the Pride.

Karolina has struggled to come to terms with her past, her Majesdanian heritage, and her desire to be happy and live a normal college life with her girlfriend. But she knows that being in the Runaways is where she is most herself. She has offered to sacrifice herself to save her teammates and her planet several times, including when under vampiric attack. Luckily, Karolina's solar blood is deadly to vampires!

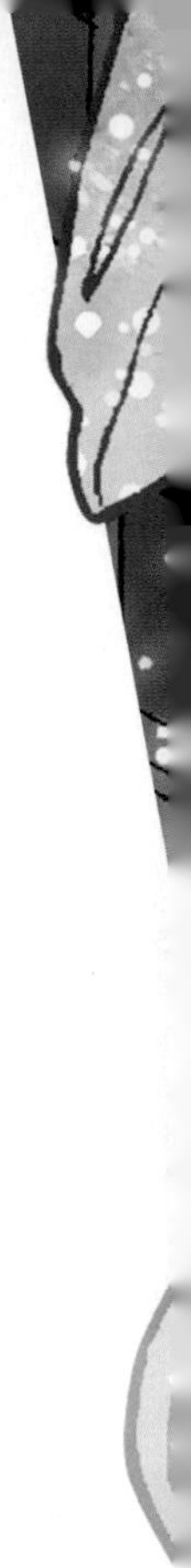

Friends, allies, and role models:
Nico Minoru (p30), **Gertrude Yorkes** (p38), **Molly Hayes** (p122)

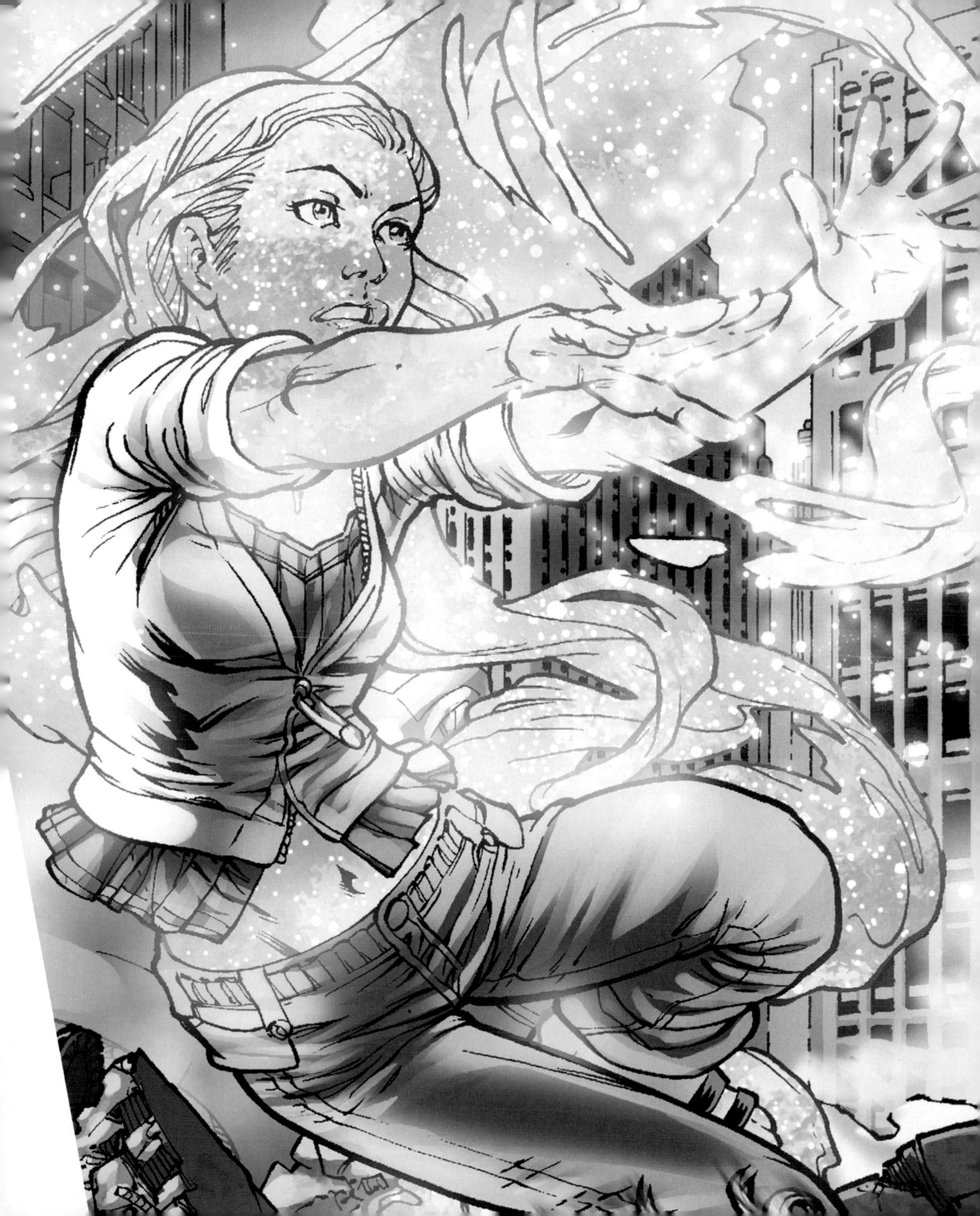

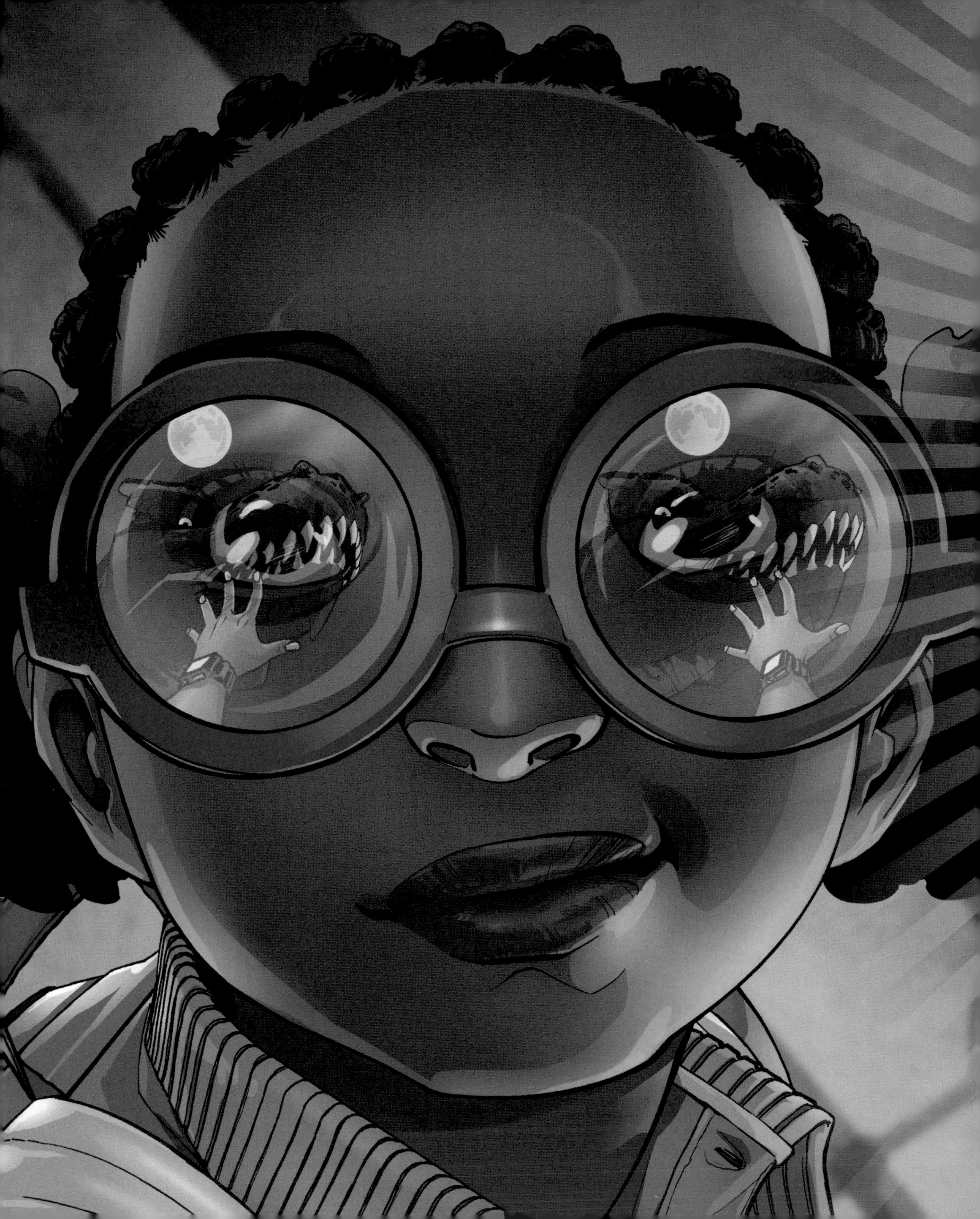

CURIOUS

Not every hero has to take up a sword and shield to bring about change. From Shuri's groundbreaking technology to Nadia's never-ending thirst for knowledge, these inquisitive and intrepid girls and women never stop looking for ways to expand their minds, hunt for information, and improve the lives of others.

◀ Moon Girl (p110)

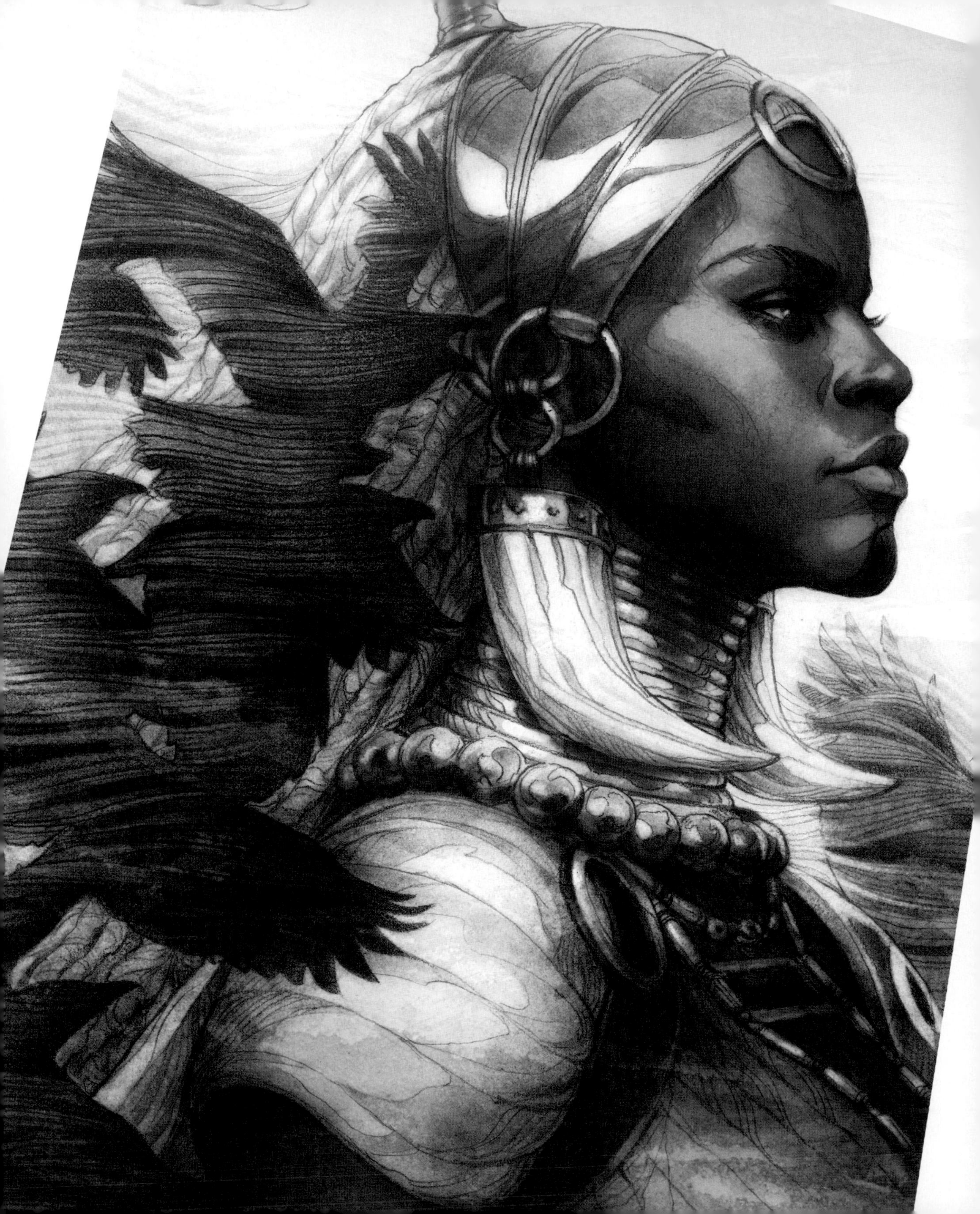

SHURI

"It's a 'mantle,' not a catsuit, thank you very much."

As King T'Challa's half-sister, Shuri is heir to the throne of Wakanda, the most technologically advanced nation on Earth. Not content with being a genius and a master of Wakandan technology, Shuri's lifelong goal was to become the first female Black Panther—the protector of Wakanda, a role earned through trials and given to those deemed worthy. She dedicated herself to this dream, training fiercely with T'Challa and the *Dora Milaje*, Wakanda's female warriors.

Shuri was more than prepared to lead the Wakandan people when her time came. Crowned queen, she was imbued with the superhuman powers that come with the successful completion of the Black Panther ritual, and even has her own Vibranium-laced suit. Through special spiritual tuition, she also gained transformative powers and super-speed. Self-assured and strong, Shuri has kept Wakanda safe from outside interference (especially against invading sea lord Namor and his army of Atlanteans) with her diplomacy in the throne room and combat skills. The only thing Shuri loves more than teasing her older brother is creating cutting-edge technology.

Friends, allies, and role models:
Storm (p16), **Black Widow** (p18), **Queen Ramonda** (p36), **Ayo** (p74)

SPIDER-WOMAN

"From now on, Spider-Woman fights back!"

Jessica Drew is a straight-talking Super Hero with spider-powers. Her parents were Hydra scientists who infused their child with a special spider-serum in order to save her from an illness. As a result, Jessica gained powers such as superhuman speed and agility, and the ability to crawl up walls. In addition, she can shoot self-generated "venom blasts" of pure energy and glide through the air.

Jessica was brainwashed into becoming a Hydra field agent, and trained in hand-to-hand combat and spying. She defected from Hydra after discovering the group's evil nature, and moved to California as "Spider-Woman," a private detective and crime fighter. Although she has also worked for S.H.I.E.L.D., S.W.O.R.D., the Lady Liberators, and the Avengers, Jessica prefers working alone. She left S.H.I.E.L.D. to continue helping individuals in need. She is now a mother, and continued investigating and battling crime throughout her pregnancy, even fighting off an alien Skrull invasion just moments after the birth of her son, Gerry. Jessica's preferred mode of transport is her classic motorcycle.

Friends, allies, and role models:
Captain Marvel (p12), **Hellcat** (p20), **She-Hulk** (p106), **Echo** (p112)

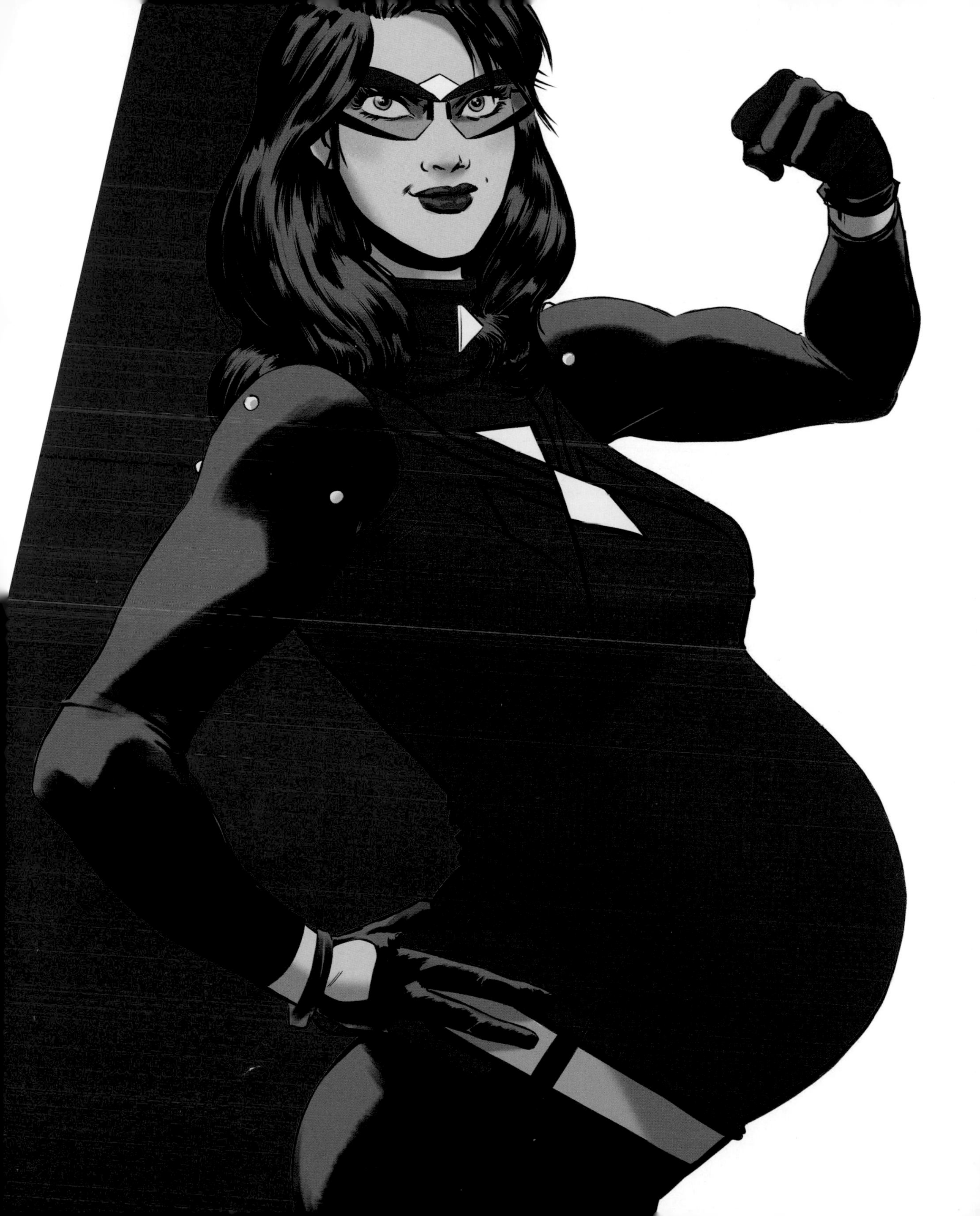

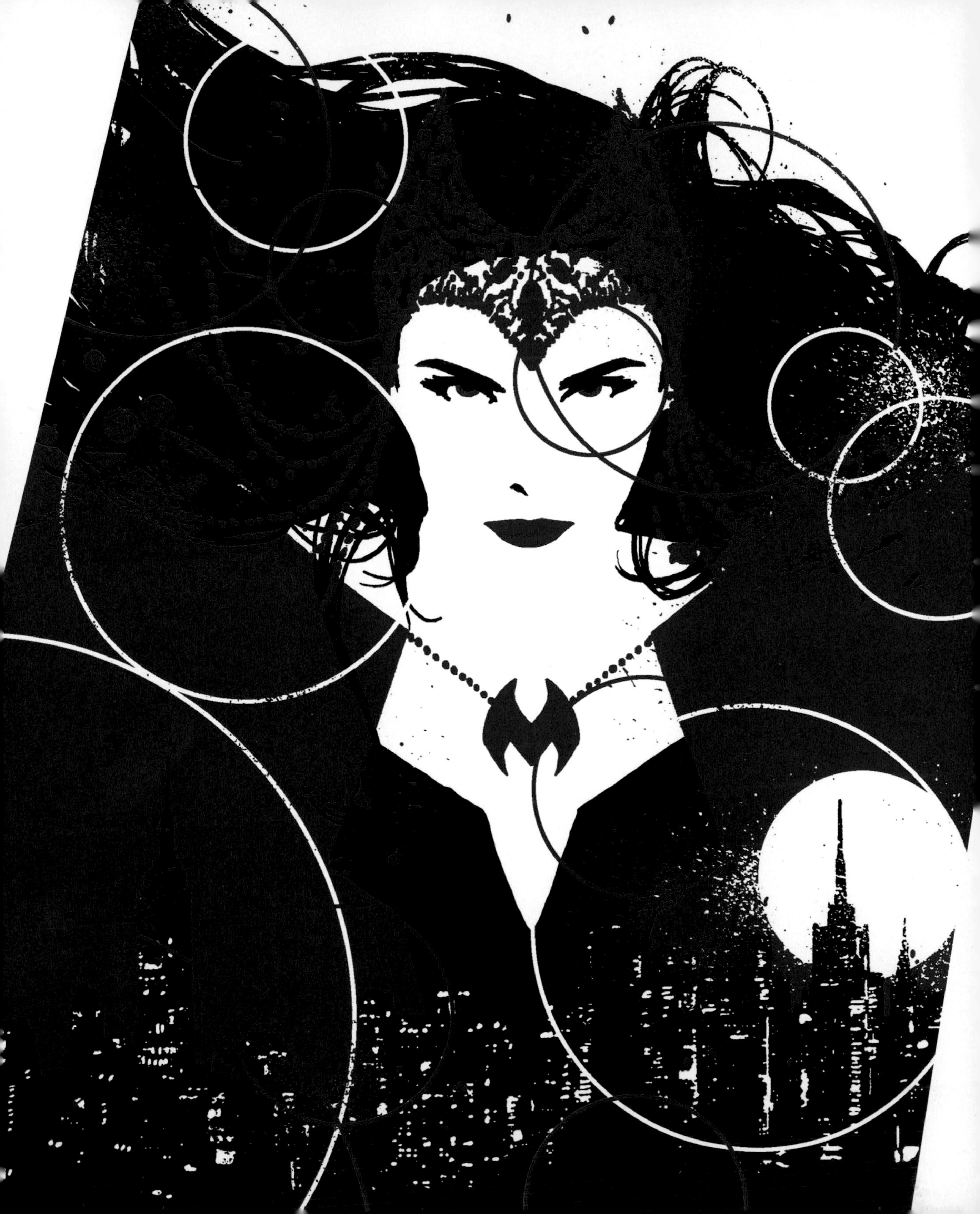

SCARLET WITCH

"Wanda Maximoff is **in the room** and **she can speak for herself."**

Wanda Maximoff is a witch whose hexes can alter the very fabric of reality. She and her twin brother, Pietro, were first recruited by Magneto into his Brotherhood of Evil Mutants, a group that believed mutants (those born with the power-bearing X-gene) were superior to humans. It was there that Wanda became known as the Scarlet Witch. Growing uneasy with the Brotherhood's ideals, Wanda and her brother flipped sides and joined the Avengers. Here she found friendship and love—she was even married to fellow Avenger, the Vision, for a time.

Wanda became a founding member of Force Works, a team of former Avengers who relied on her witchcraft to determine where crimes would be committed before they occurred. Wanda is so powerful she sometimes has difficulty maintaining control over her magic and her mind, such as the time she once caused all of reality to dissolve into a new mutant-dominated world. Now working as an occult detective in New York City, Scarlet Witch wants people to know that she is a reliable and trustworthy hero. She is also a vegetarian.

Friends, allies, and role models:
Wasp—Janet Van Dyne (p46), **Madame Web** (p70), **Mantis** (p84)

SHE-HULK

"I've learned that as long as I do something, justice will ultimately prevail. It's a test of faith... a trial of strength..."

Jennifer Walters is a renowned attorney with a law degree from UCLA (University of California, Los Angeles). She is also a hulking green rage monster! After she was hurt in a shooting, a life-saving emergency blood transfusion from her cousin, Bruce Banner, filled Jennifer with the same gamma radiation that makes him transform into the Hulk. Jennifer now transforms into She-Hulk, but unlike Bruce, she has full control during the change, keeping her intelligence and personality once transformed. Jennifer often prefers to stay in She-Hulk form; she enjoys the authority and confidence that comes with being 7ft (2.1m) tall, green, and muscular.

She-Hulk has worked with teams such as the Avengers, the Defenders, and the Lady Liberators. She now runs her own law practice in New York City (where Hellcat briefly served as her private investigator), often representing vulnerable or super-powered clients. She-Hulk uses humor to lighten tension during fights. In addition to dealing out justice and smashing things, she also loves her motorcycle, which she calls "Baby."

Friends, allies, and role models:

Hellcat (p20), **Valkyrie** (p28), **Wasp—Janet Van Dyne** (p46), **Gamora** (p48)

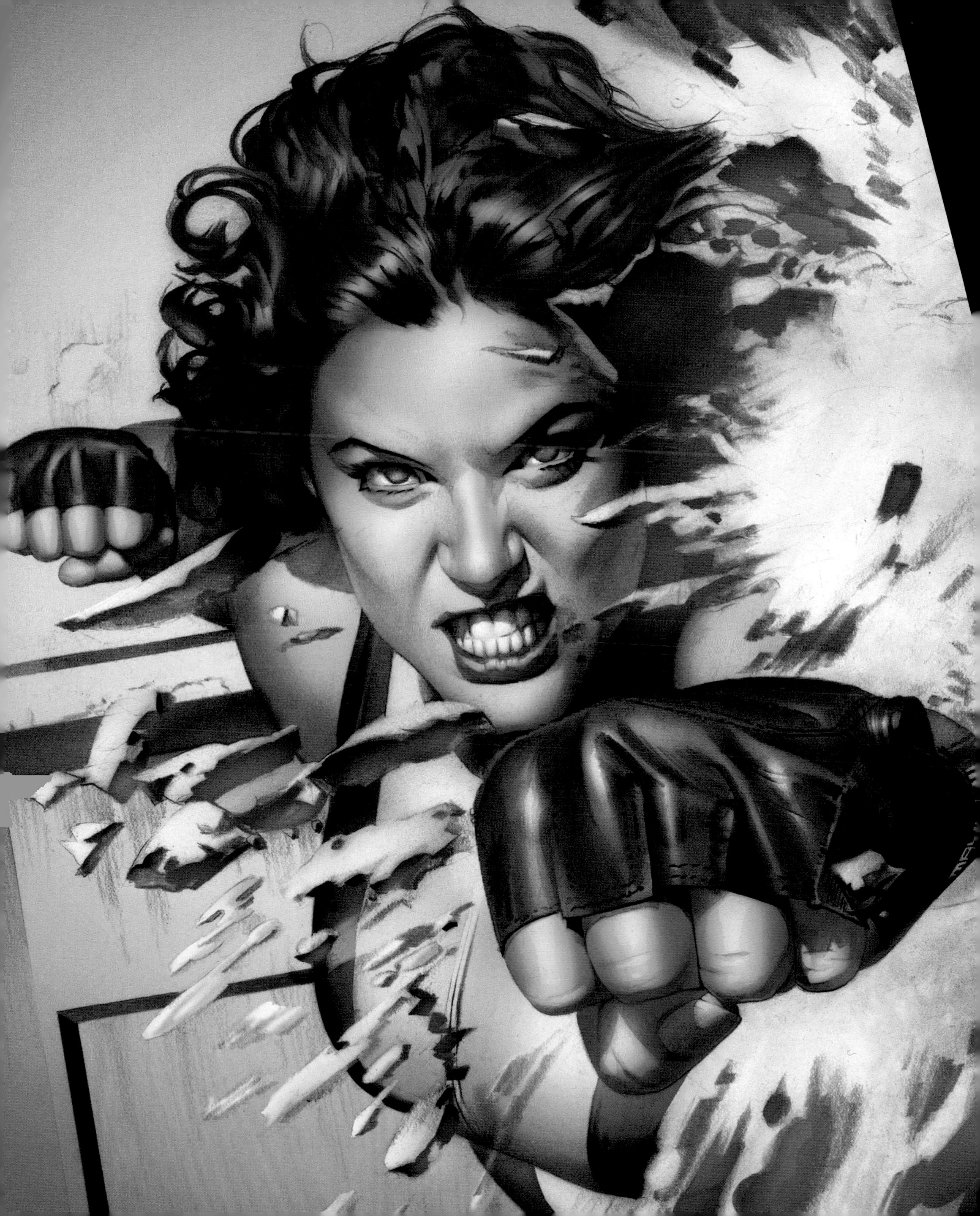

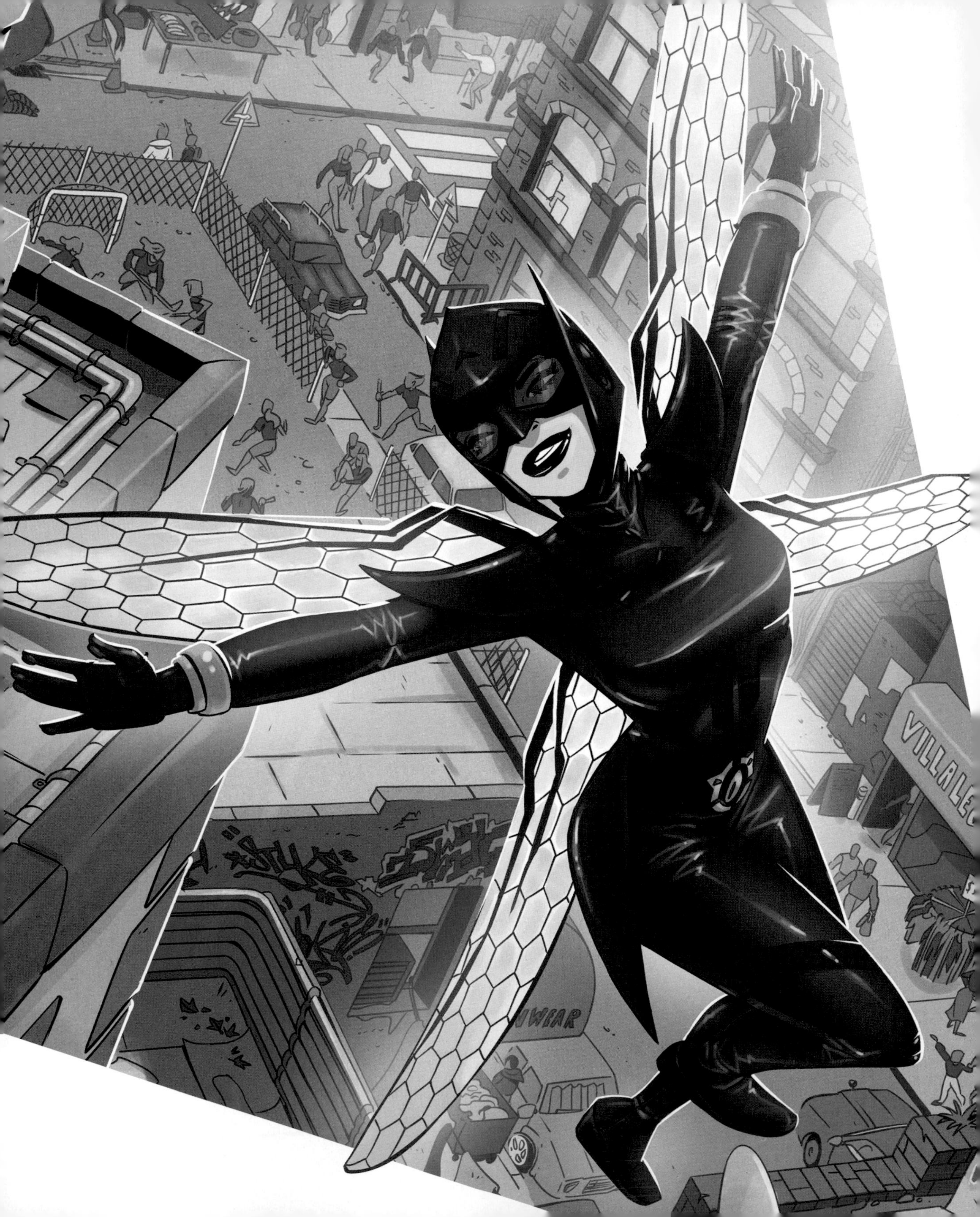

WASP

"Girls my age. Overlooked geniuses. Untapped potential. There are hundreds, maybe thousands!"

Nadia Van Dyne is nearly always cheerful, and loves to learn more about the world around her, from new food to different cultures. The daughter of scientist Hank Pym and his first wife, Maria, Nadia was kidnapped soon after her birth. She was held captive for years in the Red Room, a facility in Moscow that trained girls to become assassins. Nadia was selected for its science team due to her natural talents in chemistry, engineering, and physics. She taught herself to build shrinking technology—but then used it to escape!

Nadia later discovered her parents had sadly passed away, but she found a new mentor in Hank's second wife, Janet Van Dyne—the original Super Hero named Wasp. Nadia took Janet's surname as her own, and became the second Wasp, building her own winged suit. She is inspired by other scientists, such as the biochemist and Super Hero Bobbi Morse, aka Mockingbird. Nadia wants to encourage other girls to reach their potential, and recruits a team of fellow geniuses to join her new organization, G.I.R.L. (Genius in Action Research Labs).

Friends, allies, and role models:
Ms. Marvel, (p26), Wasp—Janet Van Dyne (p46), Snowguard (p76)

MOON GIRL

"...most people never wanted to see me as anything but a **normal little girl**... But I have **big ideas.**"

Lunella Lafayette is only nine years old, but she is officially the smartest person on the planet! Lunella's classmates tease her for being a science geek, and call her Moon Girl due to her daydreaming. Lunella carries the alien Inhuman gene in her DNA, and is desperate to find a cure. She invents amazing gadgets in her secret lab deep underneath the school.

Lunella's life changes forever when mighty red T. rex Devil Dinosaur stomps through a time portal from an alternate reality. To her surprise, the pair make an excellent crime-fighting duo, from defeating bank robbers to rescuing Manhattan's citizens. Lunella decides to use Moon Girl as her Super Hero name, jumping into action with her spring-loaded roller skates and sneeze-powder pistol. Though she finds Devil Dinosaur annoying at times (especially his snoring), they soon become the best of friends. Lunella's Inhuman genes are later activated, causing her to switch bodies with Devil Dinosaur whenever she is angry or hungry. With Ms. Marvel's help, Lunella is learning to see the positive side of being Inhuman.

Friends, allies, and role models:
Ms. Marvel (p26), **Quake** (p64), **Ironheart** (p114)

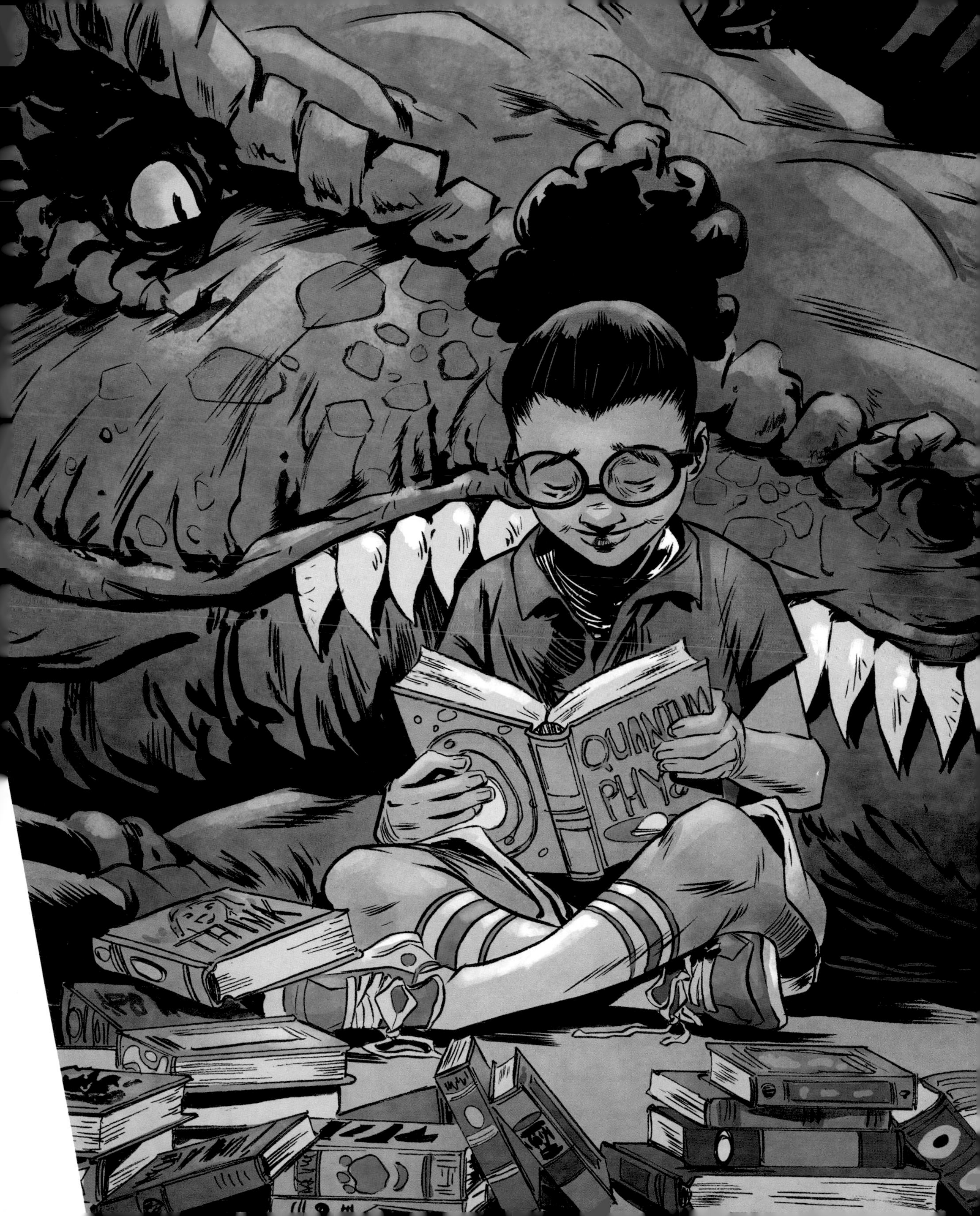
QUANTUM
PHY
THINK

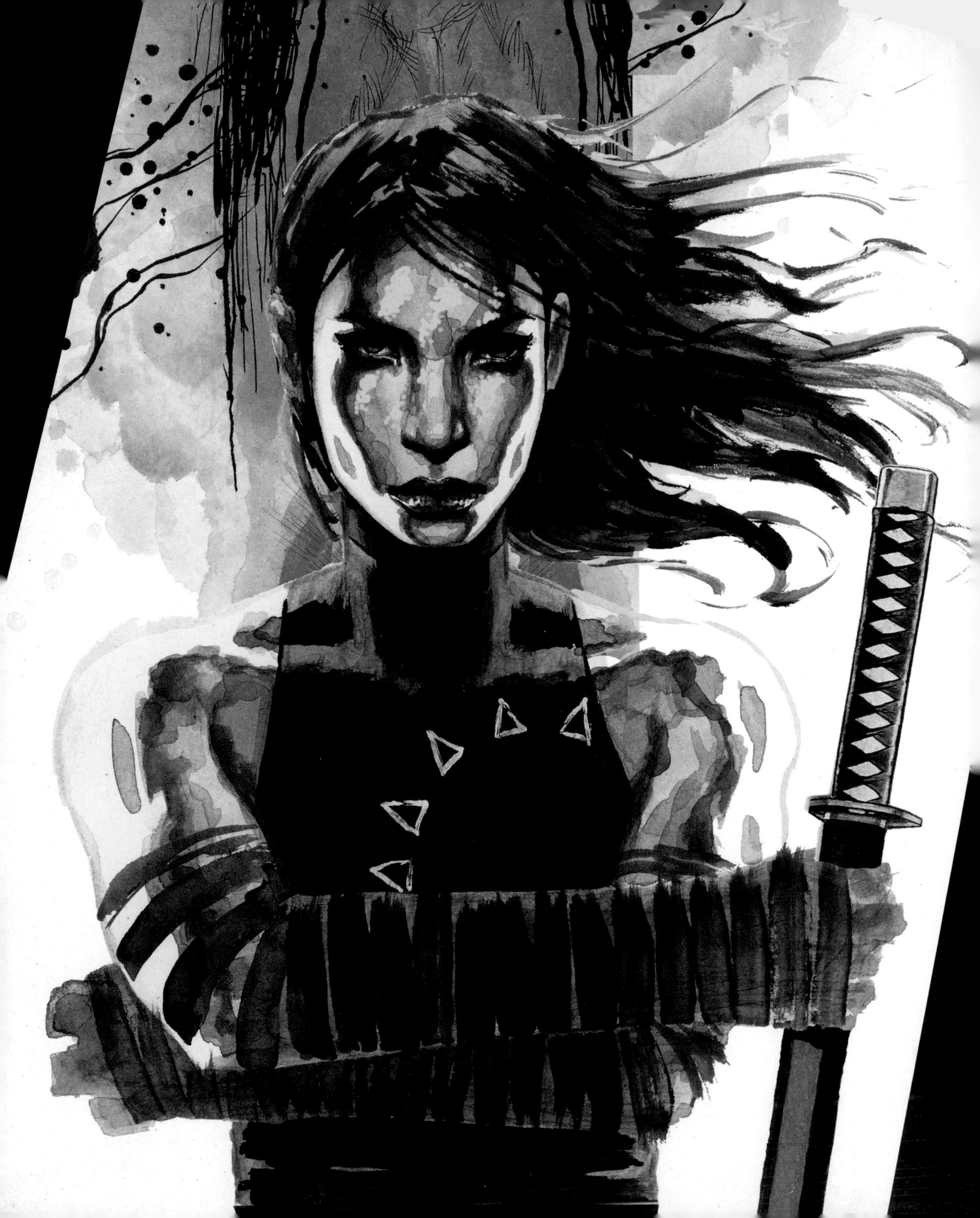

ECHO

"Hello, **villain.** I have a **performance** for you."

The Latina-Cheyenne child prodigy Maya Lopez was born completely deaf and with photographic reflexes—the ability to exactly mimic any motion she sees. This made Maya a gifted fighter and performer, excelling especially in dance and piano. Maya faced tragedy when her father, a gangster, was betrayed by the Super Villain Kingpin. She later sought to defeat Kingpin and avenge her father, taking the name Echo to disguise her identity, and bearing a white painted handprint on her face as a Super Hero "mask."

Echo moved to New York to undergo a soul-searching "vision quest"—a Native American rite of passage taken before entering adulthood. Afterward, she joined the New Avengers and took on a new secret ninja identity, Ronin. She used her mimicking powers to adopt ninja skills to halt the evil group Hydra, and Japanese ninja force, the Hand. Maya has remained a part of the New Avengers ever since (as Echo again) and continues to monitor the Hand's activities in Japan. Echo communicates using lip reading and mimickry, American Sign Language, and a method used by Native Americans to communicate between tribes.

Friends, allies, and role models:
Captain Marvel (p12), **Spider-Woman—Jessica Drew** (p102)

IRONHEART

"I'm **totally** going to be Tony Stark. **Except** for that **weird facial hair.**"

Diagnosed as a super-genius at five years old, and making Super Hero armor at 10, Chicago-born Riri Williams always wanted to be a scientist. She applied to be an astronaut at 11, won a scholarship to Massachusetts Institute of Technology at 15, and was soon building technology on campus. Riri has a fierce passion for inventing, engineering, and coding, and hates being interrupted while working. Becoming Tony Stark's protégée, she received personal tuition from him, and soon built a workable version of his Iron Man armor.

After meeting Pepper Potts—a role model to Riri due to her work at Stark Industries—Riri found herself in her first real fight, with the villain Techno Golem. Her subsequent victory brought with it a flood of public attention. She received an open invitation to join Super Hero team the Champions, and refused an offer to train with the organization S.H.I.E.L.D. on the grounds that she disagreed with their methods. Quick to act, she has an impulsive nature that once led to her being briefly declared Queen of Latveria. Riri settled on the Super Hero name Ironheart to honor the loved ones she has lost.

Friends, allies, and role models:
Mary Jane Watson (p62), **Pepper Potts** (p90), **Moon Girl** (p110)

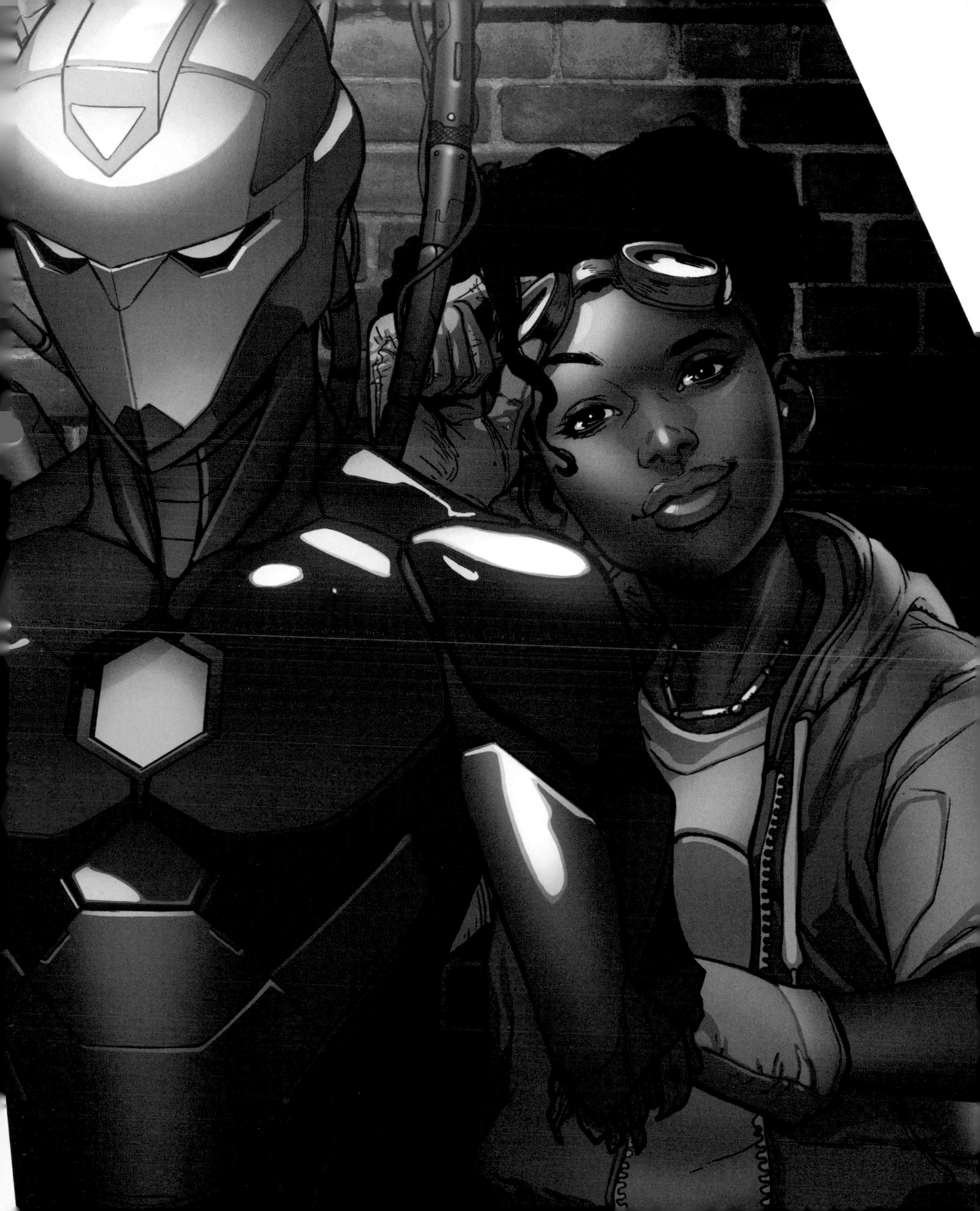

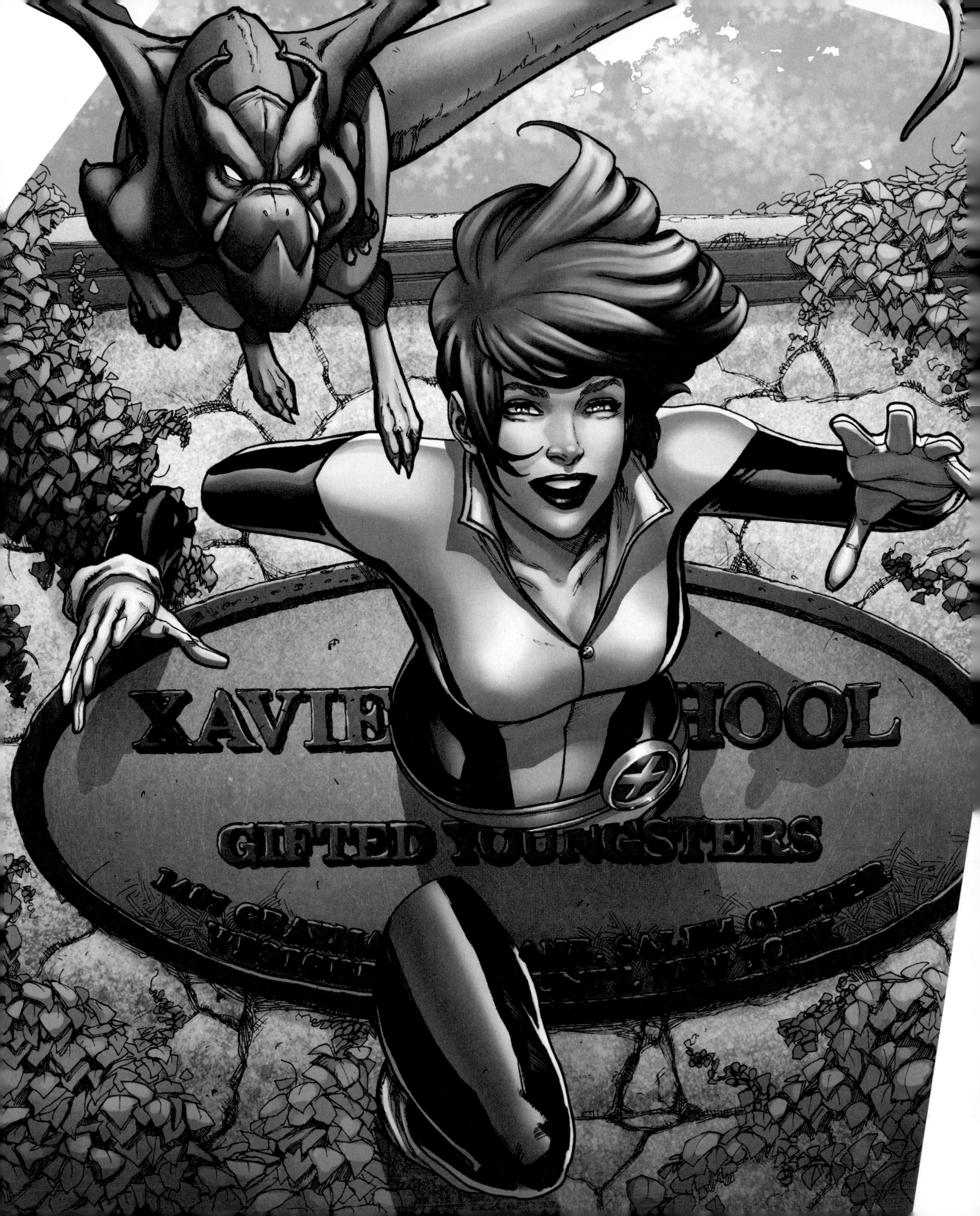
XAVIE
HOOL
GIFTED YOUNGSTERS

KITTY PRYDE

"You want to know who I am? I'm Katherine Pryde. That's the only thing that matters. The rest are just labels."

Katherine "Kitty" Pryde is a mutant whose body can phase through any solid object. An exceptionally bright Jewish child prodigy, she was recruited into the X-Men as a teenager, becoming the mutant team's youngest member. Kitty trained hard and helped the X-Men repel countless attacks from the Brotherhood of Evil Mutants, who viewed mutants as superior to all others. For a time she adopted the alias "Shadowcat."

Kitty's phasing ability makes her immune to injury and allows her to become invisible. Her most faithful companion is a purple, cat-sized, dragon-shaped alien called Lockheed, with whom she shares an empathic connection. Kitty founded a mutant team in England named Excalibur, fought alongside Wolverine in Japan, became headmistress of the Jean Grey School for Higher Learning, and has been willing to sacrifice herself for others when necessary. Kitty's childhood pet was a hamster named Peter, and she has had an affinity for people called Peter ever since. Kitty has mastered modern dance and also computer science. She is now the leader of the X-Men.

Friends, allies, and role models:
Storm (p16), **Gamora** (p48), **Rogue** (p78), **Jean Grey** (p86)

DR. TONI HO

"I can take it from here."

From time machines to force fields, there isn't much that engineering genius Dr. Toni Ho can't build. Toni was only 11 when her physicist father, Dr. Ho Yinsen, sacrificed his life to save businessman Tony Stark, who later became Iron Man. Driven by her loss, Toni excelled in computer programming and engineering at school and won a university scholarship. She gained three PhD degrees by the time she was 20!

Toni became head of engineering at A.I.M. (Avengers Idea Mechanics), an agency that carried out global rescue missions. She built her own suit of armor, working as the hero Rescue, and specialized in non-lethal weapons like gas pellets and stun lasers. A.I.M. later became American Intelligence Mechanics, and Toni joined its new team, the U.S. Avengers, as hero Iron Patriot. Toni is very hardworking, but her girlfriend Aikku Jokinen often worries Toni never gives herself a break. However, Toni keeps calm under pressure, whether she's fighting alien ships or forming an escape plan—using eyeglasses and a piece of chewing gum—to free her kidnapped boss. Her teammates are so impressed that they vote for her to be their new leader. Toni decides to stop using the Iron Patriot suit, and she later chooses to turn A.I.M. into a brand new organization named R.E.S.C.U.E.

Friends, allies, and role models:
Squirrel Girl (p82), **Ironheart** (p114)

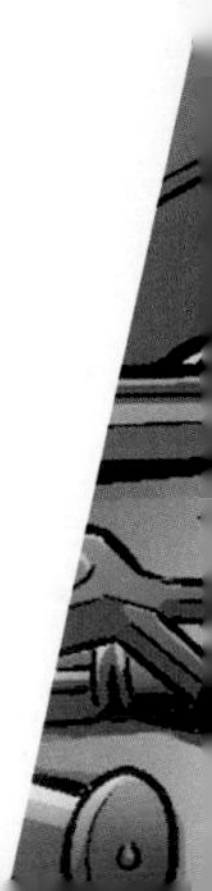

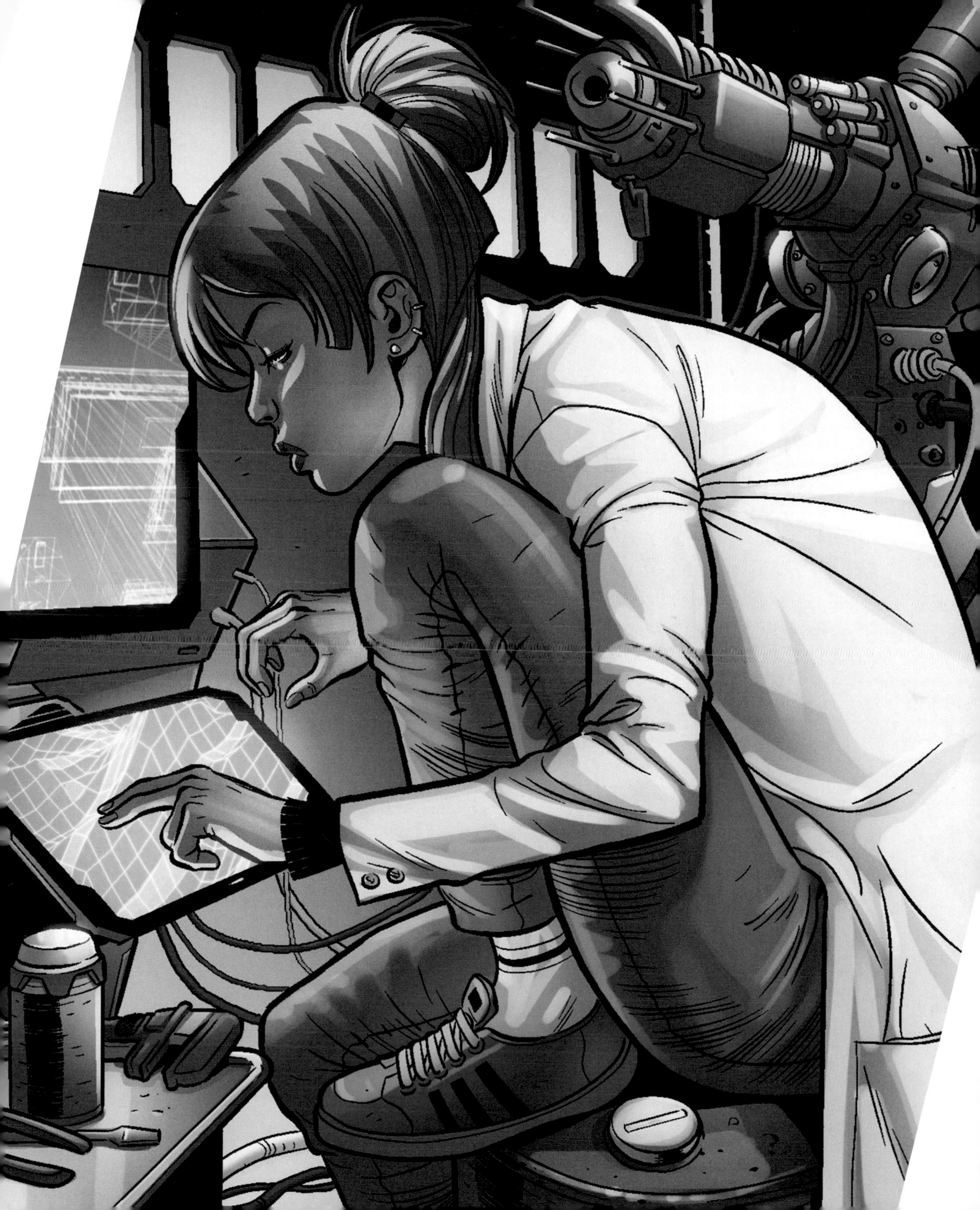

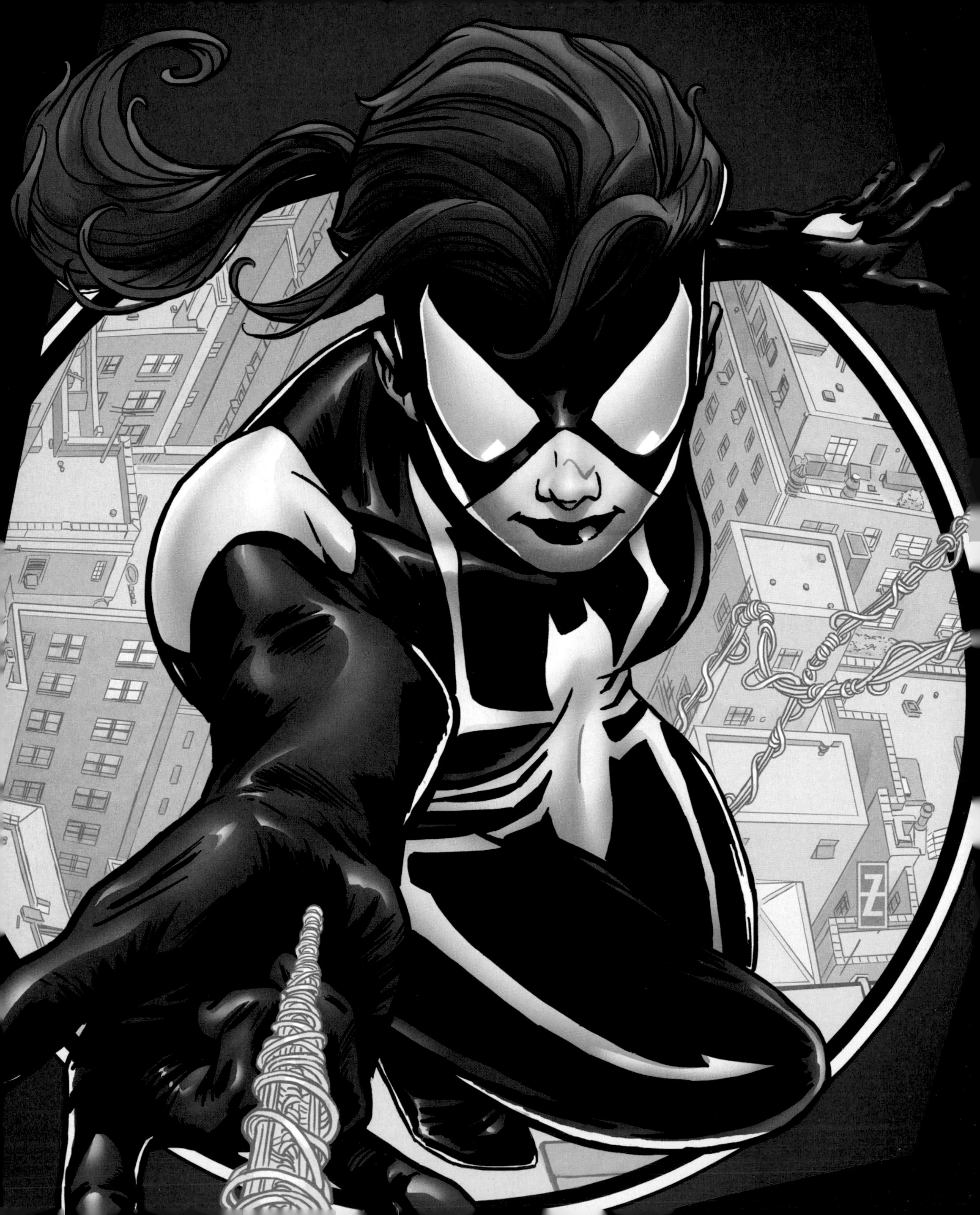

SPIDER-GIRL

"My father once told me there's no way to get a good story, to do a good job, without embedding yourself in the dirt."

Anya Corazon emigrated from Mexico to New York with her journalist father when she was very young. At her new school, she took up gymnastics. At 17, on her way home, she stopped to help a stranger under attack, using her quick reflexes to come to the rescue. The man she assisted was a member of the Spider Society, an ancient order devoted to those with spider-powers. He saw potential in his savior and showed Anya how to unlock her powers. Thanks to a special spider-shaped tattoo, she gained super-speed, agility, strength, and the power to create her own protective exoskeleton.

Going by the name "Araña" (the Spanish word for "spider"), Anya fought alongside the Spider Society to fend off those who want spider-powered people destroyed. After Spider-Woman Julia Carpenter became Madame Web, she left her old costume to Anya, who took on the name "Spider-Girl." On top of being an excellent Super Hero, Anya has kept up her gymnastics, is bilingual in Spanish and English, and is a skilled computer hacker.

Friends, allies, and role models:

Captain Marvel (p12), **Black Widow** (p18), **Silk** (p32), **Madame Web** (p70)

MOLLY HAYES

"You know I get angry when someone makes my friends cry... And you won't like me when I'm angry!"

Witty and well liked, Molly Hayes may be the youngest member of Super Hero group the Runaways, but she more than makes up for it with her mutant powers of super-strength and invulnerability—and her big and cheerful personality. Molly has fought bravely alongside her Runaways teammates, and even endured kidnapping, in order to bring down their parents' Super Villain group, the Pride. Despite knowing that her parents were deadly super-powered clones, Molly still misses them and has sought solace in school life, band practice, and a new BFF, Abigail.

Molly is not above lifting cars to prove her toughness, and her talent has led Wolverine to attempt to recruit her to the X-Men. However, Molly's loyalty lies with her friends in the Runaways and she is intuitively often the one to notice when something is wrong. Molly's abilities are not yet fully realized, and overuse of her powers can leave her in need of a nap. Her teammates affectionately gave her the Super Hero name "Bruiser," but Molly personally prefers "Princess Powerful."

Friends, allies, and role models:
Nico Minoru (p30), **Gertrude Yorkes** (p38), **Karolina Dean** (p96)

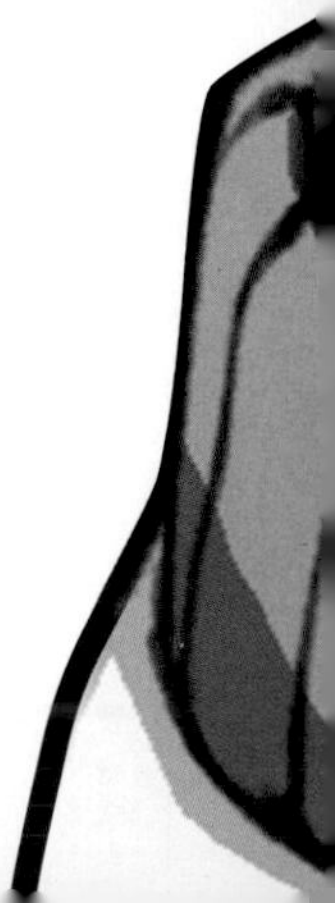

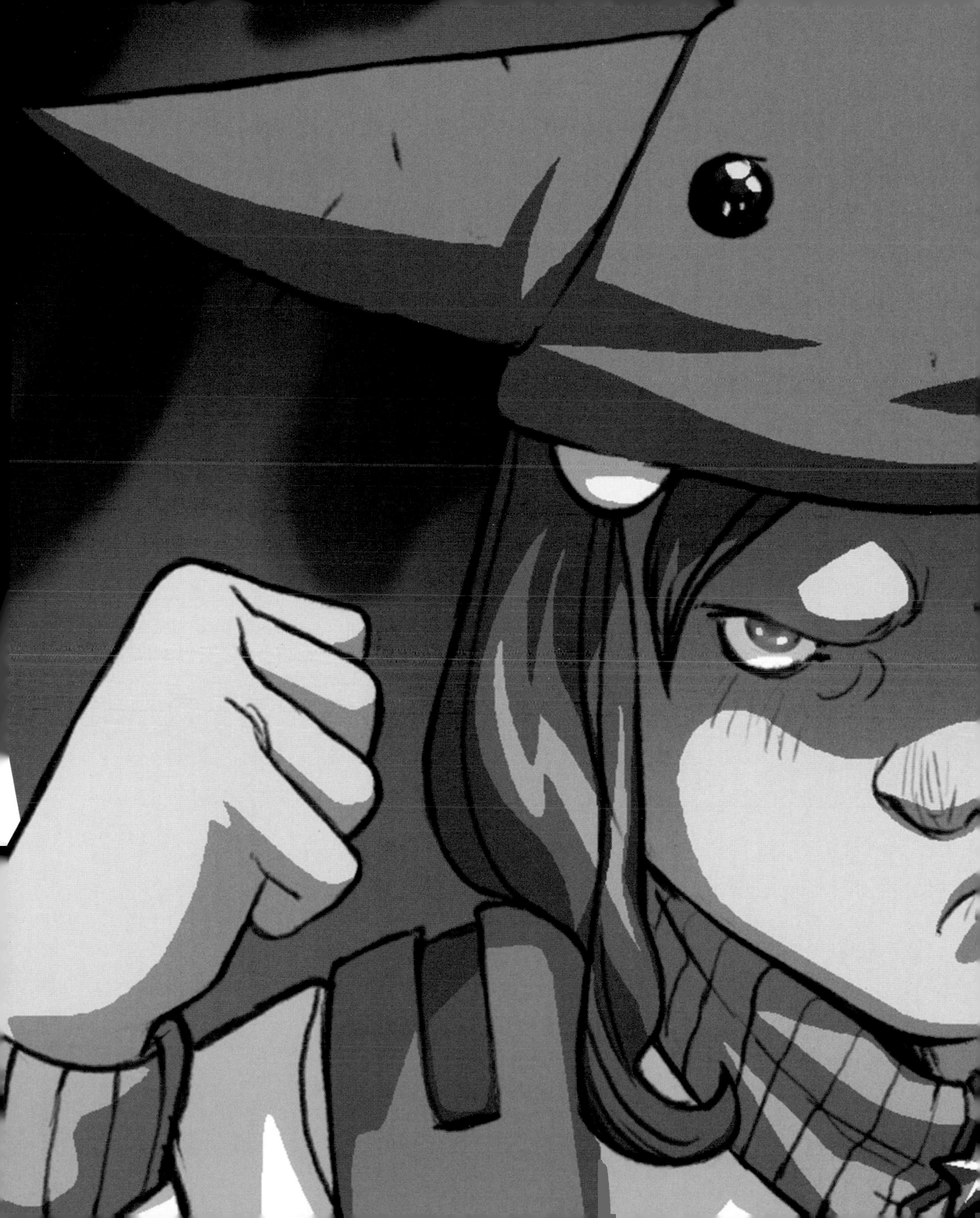

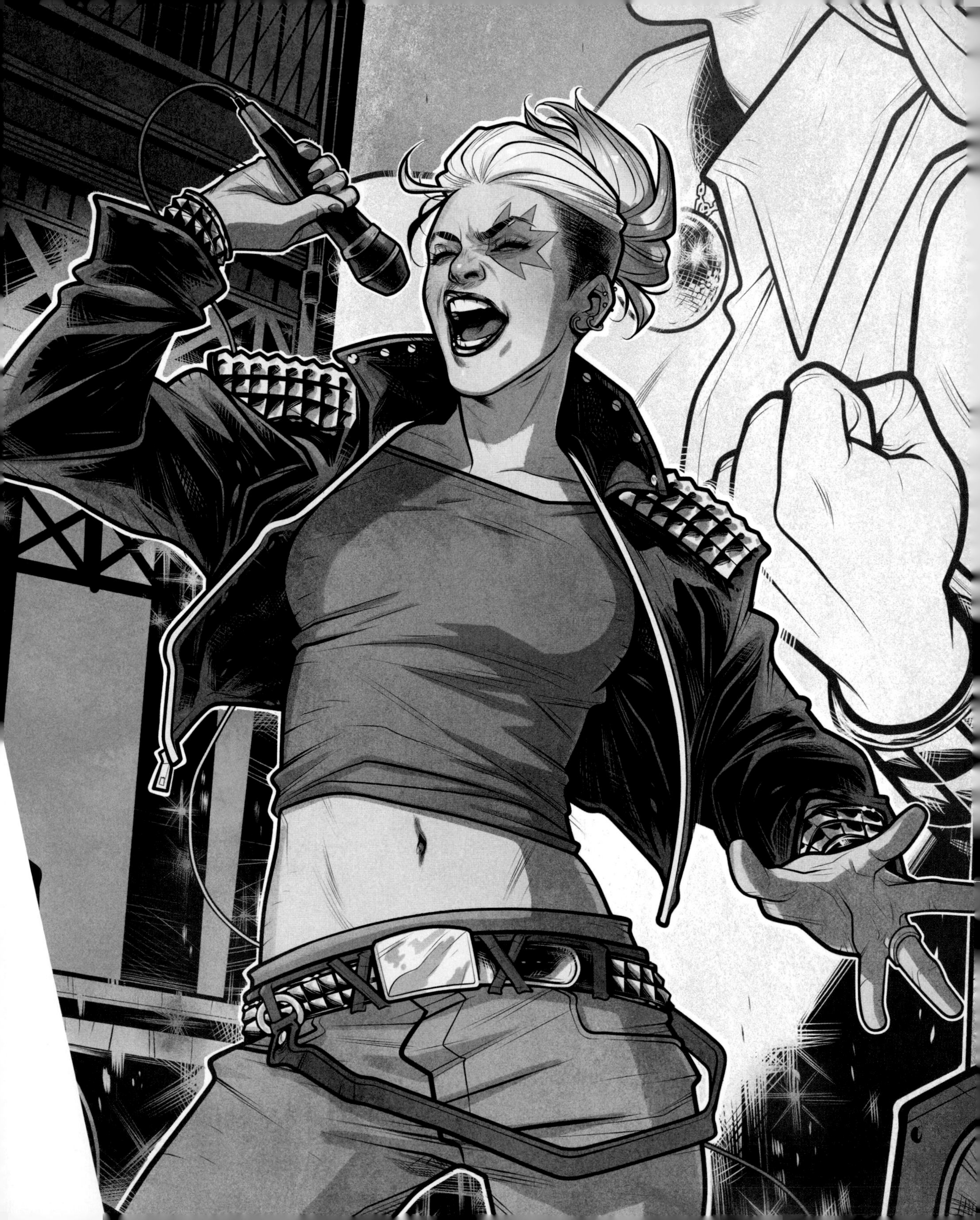

DAZZLER

"Listen. Can you hear it? This city is a symphony. And I'm her speaker."

Growing up, Alison Blaire always dreamed of becoming a singer. Her father, however, wanted her to become a lawyer. It was while she was performing that Alison discovered she had mutant powers: the ability to emit blinding light, boost the volume of her voice, produce sonic vibrations, and even fire laser beams. Keen to learn how to fully harness her powers and follow her musical dreams, Alison created her own stage costume and gave herself the name "Dazzler."

To start with, Alison used her abilities to draw people to her concerts, but she was soon noticed by the X-Men, who offered her a place on their team. Initially unwilling to abandon her singing career, Alison found herself constantly drawn into battles with Super Villains. She has since learned she can use her powers both to fight for justice and to sing. As well as joining the X-Men, Dazzler has worked as an agent for S.H.I.E.L.D. and as a member of all-female Super Hero group A-Force. But she still feels most at home wearing her customized magnetic roller skates or rocking out on stage in Brooklyn with her punk band.

Friends, allies, and role models:
America Chavez (p56), **Jean Grey** (p86), **Singularity** (p94), **She-Hulk** (p106)

GLOSSARY

alter ego: a side of someone's personality that is different, such as a secret identity.

alternate realities: separate worlds, dimensions, or universes often seemingly inhabited by the same people, but living different lives.

Asgardians: a godlike race of beings, including thunder god Thor and King Odin, from the other-dimensional world of Asgard.

Atlanteans: a race of underwater people from the kingdom of Atlantis—a small, sunken continent under the Atlantic Ocean—ruled by their king, Namor.

Attilan: the secret, moveable city home of the Inhumans, sometimes located on Earth.

Avengers: a squad of Super Heroes united to defend Earth from attacks that no hero could face alone.

Champions: a team of young Super Heroes seeking to right the wrongs committed by past generations.

Defenders: a large and often-changing team of Super Heroes fighting to protect Earth from otherworldly attacks.

Dora Milaje: Wakanda's all-female, highly trained security force.

empathy: the ability to understand and feel, or share, others' emotions.

Hydra: an ancient, evil organization seeking worldwide domination, and constantly reforming itself with new recruits.

Inhumans: a genetically enhanced race of superhumans, whose powers lie dormant until unlocked by exposure to the Terrigen Mists.

Mjolnir: a mighty, enchanted hammer, that can only be wielded by those it deems worthy.

mutant: a human born with extraordinary features or powers.

phasing: the ability to pass through solid objects.

prodigy: a child with exceptional natural talent and skills.

protégée: a girl or woman being trained in a certain subject, or area of work, by an expert.

radiation: the discharge of energy in the form of electromagnetic waves, dangerous in large amounts.

S.H.I.E.L.D.: "Strategic Homeland Intervention, Enforcement, and Logistics Division"—a secret defense organization created to protect Earth from global threats.

Super-Soldier Serum: a formula, developed for U.S. soldiers, giving those injected with it enhanced physical and athletic abilities.

S.W.O.R.D.: "Sentient World Observation and Response Department"—an intelligence agency specializing in alien threats.

telekinesis: the ability to move objects with the power of the mind.

telepathy: the ability to read other people's minds and communicate without speech or signs.

Terrigen Mists: coming from crystals, a force that is capable of unlocking powers in Inhumans, but with the potential to hurt others.

Valhalla: the Asgardian afterlife, where worthy Asgardians go when they die.

Vibranium: a rare and almost indestructible metal that can be made into weapons and suits, mined only in Wakanda.

Wakanda: a highly technologically advanced nation, located in Africa.

X-gene: the part of a mutant's DNA that naturally gives them their unusual powers or features.

X-Men: a team of mutants united to work for good by genius Professor X.

DK | Penguin Random House

Senior Editors Ruth Amos, Emma Grange
Designer Rosamund Bird
Pre-Production Producer Siu Yin Chan
Senior Producer Mary Slater
Managing Editor Sadie Smith
Managing Art Editor Vicky Short
Publisher Julie Ferris
Art Director Lisa Lanzarini
Publishing Director Simon Beecroft

Book concept by Beth Davies.
DK would like to thank Chris Gould and Lisa Sodeau
for design assistance, and Julia March for proofreading.

First American Edition, 2018
Published in the United States by DK Publishing
345 Hudson Street, New York, New York 10014

DK, a Division of Penguin Random House LLC
18 19 20 21 22 10 9 8 7 6 5 4 3 2 1
001-311495-Dec/2018

MARVEL

Published in Great Britain by Dorling Kindersley Limited.

A catalog record for this book is available from the Library of Congress.

ISBN 978-1-4654-7885-6

DK books are available at special discounts when purchased in bulk for sales promotions, premiums,
fund-raising, or educational use. For details, contact: DK Publishing Special Markets,
345 Hudson Street, New York, New York 10014
SpecialSales@dk.com

Printed and bound in China

A WORLD OF IDEAS:
SEE ALL THERE IS TO KNOW
www.dk.com

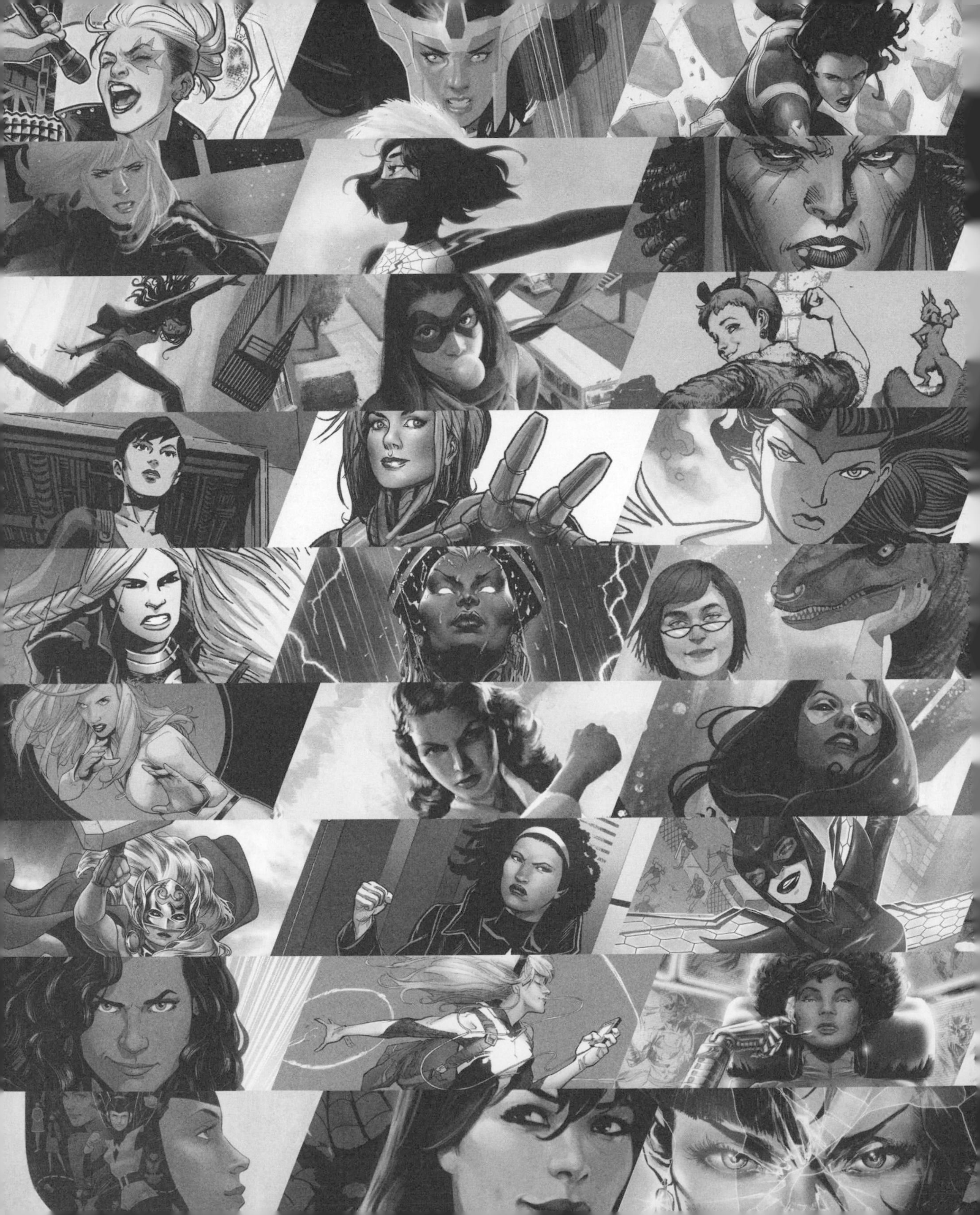